"Are you planning on telling me your name?"

Matt asked the wounded woman he'd found on the beach.

She rested her head on his car's seat back. "Wasn't planning on it, no."

"Are you being mysterious or rude?"

"Neither."

"Okay, I'll play." He took his eyes off the road long enough to catch a glimpse of her. She was struggling to remain conscious. Her long lashes fluttered against her cheek and her flawless skin had gone pale. "Keep your hand up, the bleeding has started again."

She just shrugged.

"So what am I supposed to call you?"

"Call me whatever you want. 'Hey you' is fine. It doesn't matter. It isn't as if we're about to engage in a meaningful, interpersonal relationship."

Dear Harlequin Intrigue Reader,

In honor of two very special events, the Harlequin Intrigue editorial team has planned exceptional promotions to celebrate throughout 2009. To kick off the year, we're celebrating Harlequin Books' 60th Diamond Anniversary with DIAMONDS AND DADDIES, an exciting four-book miniseries featuring protective dads and their extraordinary proposals to four very lucky women. Rita Herron launches the series with *Platinum Cowboy* next month.

Later in the year Harlequin Intrigue celebrates its own 25th anniversary. To mark the event we've asked reader favorites to return with their most popular series.

- Debra Webb has created a new COLBY AGENCY trilogy. This time out, Victoria Colby-Camp will need to enlist the help of her entire staff of agents for her own family crisis.
- You can return to 43 LIGHT STREET with Rebecca York and join Caroline Burnes on another crime-solving mission with Familiar the Black Cat Detective.
- Next stop: WHITEHORSE, MONTANA with B.J. Daniels for more Big Sky mysteries with a new family. Meet the Corbetts—Shane, Jud, Dalton, Lantry and Russell.

Because we know our readers love following trace evidence, we've created the new continuity KENNER COUNTY CRIME UNIT. Whether collecting evidence or tracking down leads, lawmen and investigators have more than their jobs on the line, because the real mystery is one of the heart. Pick up *Secrets in Four Corners* by Debra Webb this month, and don't miss any one of the terrific stories to follow in this series.

And that's just a small selection of what we have planned to thank our readers.

We'd love to hear from you, and hope you enjoy all of our special promotions this year.

Happy reading, and happy anniversary, Harlequin Books!

Sincerely,

Denise Zaza
Senior Editor
Harlequin Intrigue

KELSEY
ROBERTS

THE NIGHT
IN QUESTION

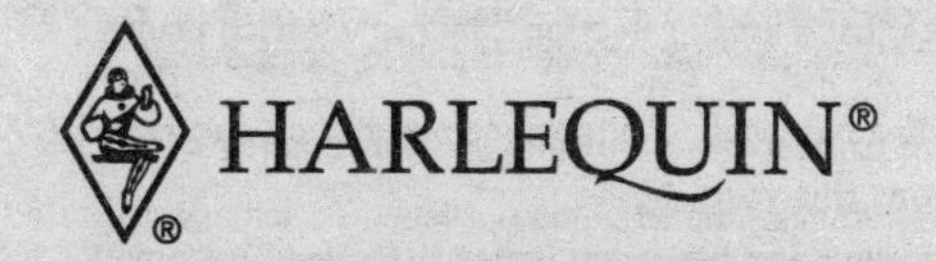

TORONTO • NEW YORK • LONDON
AMSTERDAM • PARIS • SYDNEY • HAMBURG
STOCKHOLM • ATHENS • TOKYO • MILAN • MADRID
PRAGUE • WARSAW • BUDAPEST • AUCKLAND

I'd like to thank The Nail

Recycling programs for this product may not exist in your area.

ISBN-13: 978-0-373-69376-4
ISBN-10: 0-373-69376-1

THE NIGHT IN QUESTION

This edition published by arrangement with Harlequin Books S.A.

www.eHarlequin.com

Printed in U.S.A.

ABOUT THE AUTHOR

Kelsey Roberts has penned more than thirty novels, won numerous awards and nominations and landed on bestseller lists including *USA TODAY* and the Ingrams Top 50 List. She has been featured in the *New York Times* and the *Washington Post*, and makes frequent appearances on both radio and television. She is considered an expert in why women read and write crime fiction as well as an excellent authority on plotting and structuring novels.

She resides in south Florida with her family.

Books by Kelsey Roberts

HARLEQUIN INTRIGUE

412—THE SILENT GROOM*
429—THE WRONG MAN*
455—HER MOTHER'S ARMS*
477—UNFORGETTABLE NIGHT*
522—WANTED: COWBOY*
535—HIS ONLY SON†
545—LANDRY'S LAW†
813—BEDSIDE MANNER†
839—CHASING SECRETS†
855—FILM AT ELEVEN†
886—CHARMED AND DANGEROUS†
903—THE LAST LANDRY†
921—AUTOMATIC PROPOSAL
1109—THE NIGHT IN QUESTION*

*The Rose Tattoo
†The Landry Brothers

CAST OF CHARACTERS

Kresley Hayes—What she doesn't know might very well kill her.

Matt DeMarco—Not all of this FBI agent's intentions are pure; he's got secrets of his own.

Rose Porter—Owns half of the Rose Tattoo and can't pass up an opportunity to play matchmaker.

Emma Rooper—Kresley's roommate who dies on the night in question.

Gianni—Fashion designer killed because he knows far too much.

Shelby Hunnicutt Tanner—Half owner of the Rose Tattoo who has a special secret she shares with Matt.

Janice Cross—Missing FBI agent—has she turned or is she a captive?

Hal Whiting—Coast Guard official with his fingers in lots of pies.

Chapter One

Matt DeMarco's eyesight was neon green and distorted, thanks to the night-vision goggles he was using for his fruitless scan of the horizon.

A mixture of seawater and sand sloshed around his legs as he continued a slow, methodical jog along the water's edge.

Nothing.

He'd been at it since midnight, a full twenty-seven hours since the *Carolina Moon* should have docked at Charleston Harbor. He knew enough about Atlantic tides and currents to realize that if the private yacht had experienced any sort of mechanical malfunction, it would be drifting offshore in the general vicinity of Folly Beach.

Where the hell was Janice? His softly muttered curse of frustration was lost in the sound of the gently lapping surf.

She was a damn good partner and had covered his butt, and he owed her big time. But she'd gone too far this time. Deep under cover, she'd been in the wind for over a month, not filing progress reports, not even communicating with her supervisory agent. The last report she'd filed had placed her in Charleston. And the last confirmed sighting of her was from a week ago when she'd rented a boat to take her out to the *Carolina Moon.*

Janice Cross was like a pit bull. Once she got her teeth into something, she wouldn't let go. But he prayed whatever she'd discovered on the *Carolina Moon* hadn't cost her her life.

As dawn approached, the waters were beginning to fill with the fleet of shrimpers and fishermen working the ocean, rivers and oyster beds in and around Charleston.

If the private yacht was disabled, surely one of the fishing fleet would—

His thought was lost as Matt suddenly choked in a mouthful of briny water. Only then did his brain fully process the fact that he'd tripped and gone flying into the lukewarm ocean. Spitting the grit of sand, bits of shell and God-only-knew-what-else out of his mouth, he pushed up to his knees, feeling around in the murky water for his goggles. No luck.

"Damn," he muttered, pushing dripping hair off his forehead.

Glancing over his shoulder, he looked for the cause of his dive into the shallow surf, expecting a discarded cooler or driftwood or, more likely, one of those federally protected, lumbering, loggerhead turtles that spent the month of April plodding up to the dunes to lay eggs.

The first sliver of hazy sunshine illuminated the beach, and he felt his throat squeeze tight.

This was no turtle. It was the body of a young woman whose long blond hair swished and swayed with the movement of the ebbing surf. She appeared to be wearing some kind of evening gown.

Scanning the surrounding area, Matt grabbed her beneath the arms, dragging her up higher on the beach.

Dropping to his knees at her side, he placed his ear near her mouth. Relieved to hear a single, faint wheeze, he then checked her pulse. Untangling the mass of long blond hair from her face, he tilted her head back and alternated between mouth-to-mouth and chest compressions.

When she spat out a gurgle of water, he rolled her on her side and patted her back as she coughed and sputtered water from her lungs.

Matt reached around and felt for the cell phone he kept clipped at his waistband. Flipping it open, he found himself staring at a blank screen. Sand particles crusted the keypad. His phone was state-of-the-art, but apparently not waterproof.

The woman's lashes fluttered, but her eyes still hadn't opened.

"Hang on, honey," he whispered, then again glanced in both directions. He *should* call fire and rescue and the police. Normally he would have, but his current status as a Special Agent in Charge, on loan to the short-staffed Charleston office made that impossible without blowing his unofficial assignment—finding Janice. The next best option was to hand the woman off to someone else. Janice's life might very well depend on it.

There were two guys a couple of hundred yards south. Too far away to be of any immediate help. *Crap*. He couldn't just leave her on the beach.

She coughed again, then drew in a deep, labored breath.

"I know it hurts, but you're breathing."

When she lifted her right hand, Matt noticed that blood was trickling down from her palm and also that she had a goose-egg-size lump on her forehead. Straddling her, he ran his fingers along her neck and found that aside from the fact that she wore only one gold earring, there were no bulges or obvious distensions. She didn't have a broken neck. As far as he could tell, her bloody hand was her most serious injury. Matt reached for the hem of her gown and gave a rough tug. The fabric tore easily. Though wet and sandy, as a temporary bandage for her hand it would have to do.

Spotting movement in his peripheral vision, Matt managed to shift enough to avoid the sand she flung at his face.

Though she couldn't weigh much more than a hundred pounds—wet gown included—she heaved him off her and began clawing her way toward the dunes.

He probably should have let her go. She had, after all, just ungratefully tossed him on his ass. Yep, he should just let her go on her merry way. Except that she'd nearly drowned, had a lump on her head and her hand was dripping a trail of blood onto the sand.

That, and he didn't believe in coincidences. What were the chances of Janice being missing at sea and this woman rolling in with the high tide?

Realizing she might be his only lead, Matt let out an exasperated breath and went after her. Snaking his hand around her small waist, he lifted her off the ground. She flailed against him but she didn't scream. Odd.

"Stop kicking," he said between gritted teeth, squeezing her more tightly against his chest.

"Let go. You're hurting me."

Matt loosened his grip but didn't release her. "I'm not trying to hurt you. I'm trying to help you. You're bleeding."

She stilled as he lifted her wrist and raised her hand toward her face. He heard a little breath catch in her throat.

Carefully, he reached down, hooking his hand behind her knees and lifted her into his arms. "We need to get you to a hospital. You prob—"

"No, no hospitals." Her eyes were a rich, dark blue and there was more than panic there. Matt saw a deep fear. Of what? Or who?

"My cell's useless," he told her softly, "but there's a pay phone in the parking lot." He shifted her higher in his arms as he navigated the sand. "You can call a friend."

"Pretty gallant of you given that a minute ago you were ripping off my dress," she said as she jammed an elbow into his rib cage.

Air bellowed from his lungs. "Rip your…geez,

lady! I needed something to wrap around your hand to stop the bleeding."

Confusion knitted her brows. "You weren't…?"

He glared down at her. "No, I wasn't. Call me picky, but I prefer a willing, responsive partner to a bleeding, semi-conscious one. You have to get some medical attention for that hand."

He watched as her full lips drew into a grimace as she unwound the bandage and surveyed the gash in her palm. "It doesn't look good, does it?"

Matt reached the parking lot and carried her to his Jeep. Setting her down, he leaned her against the car while he opened the passenger's door. "Who do you want me to call?"

"Call?"

It was a struggle to keep from rolling his eyes. "Either give me a name and a number or I'm taking you to the nearest emergency room."

"I told you, no hospitals."

"That wound isn't going to heal on its own." Irritation ratcheted up a notch or two. "No emergency contact number, fine. No hospital? Fine, too. Get in. I'll take you to the closest urgent-care facility. We'll make better time if I just drive you. There's a place off Calhoun Street. We can be there in twenty minutes or less. Or, Roper Hospital isn't that far. We can—"

"No," she said, shaking her head so vehemently that water splattered everywhere. "I can't—"

"—ignore that gash."

Matt knew wounds and the long, diagonal injury

to her hand was a defensive knife wound. Who had she been defending herself against and why?

"I won't ignore it. Thank you for your help."

The fact that she averted her eyes as she attempted to dismiss him didn't go unnoticed. Nor did the ridiculousness of her remark. She was still bleeding profusely, so he opted for a different tack.

He knew his own motivation for not drawing the attention of the local authorities. What he couldn't fathom was why a woman who'd obviously been in some sort of altercation, obviously jumped or been thrown into the ocean, was so resistant to going through normal channels. Seriously strange behavior.

Tugging his T-shirt over his head, he ripped off a strip of damp cotton and created a second makeshift pressure bandage.

"Thank you." She kept her elbow bent and her hand above her heart and then took a wobbly step away from the car.

Matt grabbed her by the shoulders, steadying her and preventing her from wandering off. "You should see a doctor," he reiterated.

"It's not bleeding as much," she said, lifting her hand in front of his face.

Maybe her weird reaction had something to do with the big bump on her forehead. "You need stitches, a CT scan of your head and you've likely got water still in your lungs. You don't want me to take you to the hospital, okay. Tell me who to call and you can be their problem."

"Is there a third option?"

He read fear and confusion in her eyes as she tilted her face to his. "Like?" He let the word dangle in the air between them.

"I don't have anyone to call and I can't go to a hospital, either."

Matt knew trouble when he saw it and as a rule, did his best to avoid it when possible. One look at the drenched blonde with the wide, frightened eyes and he knew *possible* had just taken a vacation.

"What boat were you on?" he asked.

"Boat?" she repeated as if he'd spoken in tongues.

He looked down at her pricey-looking stilettos, which had remained on her feet despite what she'd been through, and said, "You aren't a mermaid. So I'll assume you ended up in the water the old-fashioned way."

"Swimming?"

He actually chuckled at her deadpan delivery. "Most women don't swim in an evening gown and heels. You must have gone overboard." His mind raced forward. "There haven't been any reports of a man—*person*—overboard or vessels in distress to the Coast Guard," he said. "Did you go out alone? Capsize, maybe?" He grabbed her good hand and turned it palm up. "You've been in the water a long time," he said as he pressed gently to test the loose skin on her uninjured hand.

"How long?" she asked, and then snatched back her hand to cover her mouth as a raspy cough rumbled in her throat.

"You don't know?"

Her eyes narrowed slightly and sparkled with a flash of what might be anger. "Forgive me, but I guess I lost track of time while I was losing blood, fighting currents and floating in the ocean *in the dark.*"

She began to slouch and he tightened his arm around her waist. "How about you sit down before you fall down?"

"That might be a good idea," she agreed, putting up no resistance as he guided her into the car.

Matt lifted her legs and tucked them into the footwell before he walked around the car. On his way to the driver's seat, he grabbed a fresh shirt out of the back of the Jeep and shrugged it over his head before slipping behind the wheel. He shot her a glance as he stuck the key in the ignition. She looked like a drowned rat.

What do you know? He thought again about Janice.

"Where are we going?"

"You don't want to go to a hospital. I'm giving you that. But we're getting you appropriate medical attention."

"How?"

"A friend of a friend. I'm Matt DeMarco, by the way."

"Matt DeMarco."

Again, she seemed to be taking the words for a trial run.

Matt drove quickly back toward Charleston,

sometimes ignoring traffic signals and often weaving through cars even if it meant violating no passing zones and rolling through stop signs. "You, ah, seem a little out of it," he said softly. "Sure you don't want to rethink the hospital option?"

"Definitely not." She shifted straighter in the seat. "I appreciate what you've done, but you can just drop me at the next corner."

"Right," he scoffed. "Do you really want to roam the streets of Charleston bleeding? What do you suppose the folks would make of that?"

Matt veered to the right to cross the Ashley River. On the other side of the bridge, he could see the Battery, a jutting peninsula where the Ashley and Cooper rivers joined. If you were from Charleston—which he wasn't—you'd smugly proclaim that the Ashley and the Cooper met to create the Atlantic Ocean.

"Are you planning on telling me your name?"

She rested her head on the seat back, "Wasn't planning on it, no."

"Are you being mysterious or rude?"

"Neither."

"Okay, I'll play." He took his eyes off the road long enough to catch a glimpse of her. She was struggling to remain conscious. Her long lashes fluttered against her cheeks and her flawless skin had gone pale. "Keep your hand up, the bleeding has started again." Given the head injury, he decided it was a good idea to keep her talking. "You've got the accent, so you're a native?"

She just shrugged.

"One thing I've learned in my short time here is Southerners are rarely rude to strangers and *never* rude to strangers offering aid and comfort. So what's the deal? Your ancestors get tossed out of the Confederacy or something?"

"Or something. Who's this friend?"

"My boss's niece, actually," Matt said. "Dr. Kendall Revell. She's a pathologist and very nice."

"Pathologist?" She raked her fingers through her damp, tangled hair. "Don't they do autopsies?"

"Yep."

"Oh well, I guess that beats a vet."

Matt smiled as he turned onto Calhoun Street. "Roper Hospital is just ahead, final opportunity to change your mind."

"No thanks."

"So what am I supposed to call you?"

"Call me whatever you want. 'Hey you' is fine. It doesn't matter. It isn't as if we're about to engage in a meaningful, interpersonal relationship."

Her choice of language was telling. She was definitely educated. "'Hey you?' If you won't tell me your name, perhaps you'd like to share what you do for a living."

When he didn't get a response, he glanced over to find her slumped in the seat, unconscious.

"Freaking hell."

THE FIRST THING she noticed when she opened her eyes was the smell. A sickly mixture of alcohol, fruity air freshener and formaldehyde. The second thing was the temperature. It was freezing cold. As soon as she opened her eyes, she squeezed them shut again. A large, round reflective light hung from the ceiling just above her bed.

Her entire left side as well as her hand throbbed so she used the tips of her right fingers to explore the bed. Only it wasn't a bed, it was a cold metal slab. Her fingers grazed her hip under a light cloth and she realized she was naked. No wonder she was so cold.

Turning her head to one side, she peeked through her lashes. Satisfied that she was safe from the harshness of the bright light, she looked around and discovered she wasn't alone. Nor was she the only one wearing nothing but a sheet. She was, however, the only one not sporting a toe tag. She was in a morgue.

Completely creeped out, she pressed the sheet to her chest and had started to sit up when she felt hands close on her shoulders. At the unexpected contact, she shrieked.

"Calm down, Hey You," Matt said from behind her.

"Geez, you scared me senseless." Tilting her head back, she saw Matt wasn't alone. He was standing next to a small woman wearing surgical scrubs, a badge with her name and photo on it clipped to the shirt.

"I'm Dr. Revell," she said. "Lie still, I don't want you to pull those sutures. It took me the better part of an hour to stitch up your wounds."

"Wounds? Plural?" Her eyes darted between Matt and the doctor.

"It took thirty stitches to close the cut on your hand and another half dozen after I dug the bullet out."

Matt shrugged apologetically. "Guess I missed it. It was a small-caliber slug that entered near your armpit and lodged just under the skin."

"Technically, I'm required by law to report all gunshots to the authorities," Kendall said.

Her whole body tensed. Reaching up with her good hand, she was so terrified and confused that she grabbed a fistful of the hem of the doctor's scrub top. "Please don't do that."

"Then give me a good reason why I should risk my medical license."

Her head was spinning with images that wouldn't stop long enough for her to actually collate the fractured memories. She had no idea why, just that she couldn't let Matt or Dr. Revell call the authorities. "Reporting it won't do any good. I don't remember being shot." In unison, Matt and Dr. Revell gave her a yeah-right kind of sneer. "I'm telling the truth. I don't remember any of it."

"Then I guess you can't explain this, either," Matt said, holding up a strip of something textured, twisted and gunmetal gray.

"What is it?"

"Duct tape."

She pressed her fingers to her temple. "No, I can't explain it. Where did it come from?"

"It was wrapped around your rib cage. Or at least it was once," Matt explained. "I'm guessing the salt water got to whatever you had taped to yourself beneath your dress. And you don't remember that part, either?"

"Sorry," she mumbled.

"Then we'll start with what you do know," Matt said, his tone forceful, demanding and definitely intimidating as he came around so she didn't have to look at him upside down. "What's your name?"

She lowered her gaze, fixing it on the triangle shape formed by her feet beneath the sheet. "I can't help you with that, either."

"What?" Matt practically barked.

She started to shake and tears welled in her eyes. In a voice that managed to be vulnerable and agitated at the same time, she said, "I don't know how I ended up in the ocean wearing that gown. I have no idea how I cut my hand. Until a few minutes ago, I didn't even know I'd been shot. I have no clue who I am." She wiped at the tears as they tumbled down her cheeks

Matt asked, "What *exactly* is the last thing you remember?"

"Waking up on the beach and seeing your face."

Chapter Two

She cried tears of frustration with a healthy dose of fear. The frustration stemmed from the obvious—why couldn't she remember her own name? The fear was a little less pellucid. For some God-only-knew reason, she kept hearing a woman's voice in her head saying, 'Trust no one.' She didn't recognize the voice nor did her mind's eye bring forth an image.

She was shaking, trying hard to remember something, hell, *anything:* an address, her name, her favorite color. Anything.

"I'm going to give you an injection," Dr. Revell said, holding a syringe and squirting a quick stream of colorless liquid out of the hollow needle. "It will calm you down," she explained.

"Dr. Revell, I—"

"Call me Kendall," she insisted as she brought the needle closer. "This may hurt, I'm a little bit out of practice," the woman said with a kind smile.

She felt a pinch, then almost instantly her nerves calmed. "Why would someone shoot me?" She heard her own words slur slightly. She tried to lift her wounded hand but it felt like it weighed about three hundred pounds, so she gave up. "Or cut me?" Next she tried to sit but couldn't manage it. "I need to leave," she said.

"Why?" Matt asked.

Slowly, she shook her head. "I don't know why, just that I can't go to the authorities."

Reaching into his back pocket, Matt flipped open a soggy wallet. "Too late," he said. "I'm with the FBI."

She felt a wave of terror crash down on her. "Am I a criminal or a fugitive?"

"Let's roll your fingerprints and see," he said almost conversationally.

Kendall then inked each of her fingers onto a card. She handed the card to Matt. "We can use the computer in my office," Kendall said. Patting her charge on the shoulder, the doctor said, "You rest. Sometimes it takes a good long while for IAFIS."

"I...A—"

Kendall gave her a reassuring smile. "Integrated Automated Fingerprint Identification System. Put your head back and rest."

Easy for her to say. The doctor wasn't the one with the bullet hole and the knife wound. She bent her arm and covered her eyes from the harsh glare from the light. "Think," she demanded of her foggy brain. A face blinked into focus for a nanosecond. A tall brunette, impeccably dressed, with short hair. Her sister? Her neighbor? Her victim? She felt hot tears in the corners of her eyes.

An FBI agent? What were the chances? *If only I'd been found by an old lady out shelling or an old man sweeping the beach with headphones and a metal detector? Nope, I have to get an FBI agent.* "Matt DeMarco," she whispered.

As her hand went to her throat, an image came back with crystal clarity. Two boats, far enough away that their searchlights couldn't reach her as she clung to the barnacle-encrusted buoy. She remembered the wide arc of the beams reflecting off the small swells. And strobing red. The latter part made no sense.

Neither did not remembering her own name. Or where she lived. Or if someone loved her or vice versa. What could have happened to erase her memory? It had to be big. Major. And based on her new terror of authority figures, bad.

"KRESLEY HAYES," Matt said before they headed for his Jeep sometime later.

"I'm sorry," she said as she concentrated on not swaying as she walked. "Is that supposed to mean something?"

"It's your name."

Matt was smiling. She stopped suddenly and looked up into his gray-blue eyes. They were rimmed with inky lashes that matched his black hair.

"Hungry?"

"I'm not exactly presentable," she said, lifting the top edge of the surgical scrubs Kendall had been kind enough to supply. The doctor had also provided a sports bra and some Crocs. The only problem was

Kendall was two inches taller and a size smaller. The pants, which were rolled up at the hem, and the top were like a second skin.

"What?" she demanded.

"You really don't know who you are, do you?"

"I've been telling you that for hours and it's only now sinking in? How did you find out my name so quickly?" she asked. *And why doesn't it sound at all familiar?*

"I hit the national databases. Nothing. So I had a friend run your prints locally."

Her heart skipped. "My prints are in the system? Am I a felon or something?"

He chuckled. "No, you're a teacher. Or at least you were. Second grade. A police background check with fingerprints is standard procedure for everyone dealing with children. You would have undergone that before you were hired."

"What did I do? Fail someone so they shot me and stabbed me?"

"You haven't been a classroom teacher for a couple of years. So I think we can safely rule out an unhappy second grader. Currently, you're working toward a graduate degree in child psychology."

"You have no idea how maddening this is," she said, her voice cracking. "You got all that information from my fingerprints?"

"And my secret decoder ring."

"Very funny. Where do I live?" Kresley asked, waiting, *praying* for something that sounded familiar.

"You've got an apartment on Isle of Palms," he said.

"Thank you for taking me home," she said.

"I hope you don't mind, but I've got to make a stop first."

She did mind a little. Maybe if she walked into her own apartment her memory would break through the dam and come flooding back. Apparently patience wasn't one of her virtues. "Where are we stopping?" she asked.

"The Rose Tattoo." He hesitated for less than a second. "I'm tending bar there part-time."

"FBI pay is that bad?"

He laughed as he turned on East Bay Street. "No. I know one of the owners. I needed a cover for a personal matter, so I tend bar. Here we are," Matt said as he turned down an alley and parked between a large home and a smaller building.

"Where's here?" she asked, uneasy when she counted four other cars in the crushed-oyster-shell lot.

"The Rose Tattoo."

"It looks more like a private residence."

He turned and offered a smile. Her eyes were drawn to his mouth and she experienced a strong, brief and inappropriate millisecond of desire.

"It hasn't been a private residence since just after the Civil War," he explained. "It sat empty for a while, then it was a speakeasy during prohibition. The previous owners renovated it as a bar and lived on the second floor. Then Rose Porter bought it and was on the verge of bankruptcy until Shelby Tanner bought in."

Reaching across her to grab the door handle, his forearm brushed her belly and Kresley felt a quick zing of excitement spread through her body. His hair smelled like the ocean, but the woodsy scent of cologne still lingered on his skin.

"Hang on, I'll come around and help you."

When Kresley stepped out of the car, her knees buckled and if Matt hadn't been there to catch her, she would have folded like an accordion.

His hands grabbed her waist. Leaning back against the Jeep, she took several deep breaths to fend off the rapid pounding of her heart. Not an easy task with Matt's square-tipped fingers resting lazily on her skin.

"I'm good," she said, placing her palms on his chest. Her intention was to gently push out of his grasp. But the feel of solid muscle and the thump of his heart beneath her touch only served as a greater enticement.

Am I always this aware of a man? she wondered. *Or is it just* this *man? And could my timing be any worse?* Not having a memory was inconvenient, to say the least.

"C'mon," he said, wrapping one hand around her waist to lead her to the door marked Deliveries Only.

Together, they entered the kitchen. A woman wearing chef's whites with the name *DeLancey* embroidered on the left side of her jacket didn't even look up from chopping carrots. "Hey," she said casually, as if a strange woman with tangled hair, wearing ill-fitting scrubs was an everyday occurrence.

"Hi," Matt said as they walked the length of the sparklingly clean kitchen.

The smells had Kresley's mouth watering. The scents of garlic, onions, smoky bacon and herbs surrounded her as she neared the exit.

The dual doors were stainless steel with round windows at eye level. Kresley stopped dead in her tracks as an image flashed in her mind. Portholes. Her steps faltered and she put out a hand to brace herself on a nearby countertop. She'd looked out a porthole and seen…something.

She started to shake and perspiration coated her body.

"You're whiter than pale," Matt said, grabbing a kitchen towel to blot the sweat from her face and neck. "Are you in pain?"

Kresley shook her head. Her chest was tight and her throat had turned into a vise.

"What is it?" he asked, concern etched in the lines by his eyes.

"I wasn't supposed to go near the portholes."

"What do you remember? What triggered the panic attack?"

"The round window."

"That's all you got?"

"Yep. A flash. A snippet. I could see the porthole. I moved forward to look out, then nothing."

Matt's splayed fingers at the center of her back urged her through the doors. In the wood-panelled dining room there were ornate carvings on the molding and the edge of the horseshoe-shaped bar.

More than a century's worth of varnish polished the bar to a bright sheen. Kresley guessed the worn knotty-pine floors were original to the building. More than three dozen tables in varying sizes were arranged around the room. Each place setting included a charger, a plate and a pink napkin folded into a triangle and secured with a silver ring embossed with a rosebud.

They passed a flight of stairs guarded by ficus trees. Several ferns hung from baskets suspended from the low ceiling.

Matt helped her up on one of the leather barstools, then went around behind the bar and took out a menu.

"Let me get you some water. Then pick whatever you'd like," Matt said. "DeLancey will whip it up in minutes. I know Kendall gave you that IV but it's been some time since you ate."

"But the restaurant isn't open," she said, glancing at the closed sign in the window.

"We open for lunch in thirty minutes. Besides, DeLancey lives to cook."

"Tuna salad," Kresley said, selecting what she thought would be the easiest of the mixture of traditional southern dishes and trendy cuisine for DeLancey to prepare.

Matt poured her a glass of water, placed a lemon on the rim, and then asked, "Will you be okay for a minute while I take your order to the kitchen?"

"Sure."

Kresley rolled her neck around on her shoulders, fighting the fatigue that was quickly replacing the adrenaline. Folding her arms and resting them on the bar, she felt the sutures pull. Ignoring the mild discomfort, she placed her head on her arms and closed her eyes.

She must have dozed off for a second because she jerked upright when she felt a poke on her shoulder.

"Sorry."

Spinning on the barstool, Kresley found herself looking at a stunning woman with black hair, piercing blue-gray eyes and a warm smile. "I can explain," Kresley said on a rush of breath.

"No need. I'm Shelby Tanner," she said. "Matt spoke with my husband while you were getting stitched up. How do you feel?"

There was something awfully familiar about Shelby. "Have we met before?"

"I don't think so. Is Matt getting you something to eat?"

Kresley nodded. "He's been very kind."

"He's a good guy," Shelby agreed. "Looks like you could use some proper clothes."

Kresley looked down at her too-tight scrubs and sighed heavily. "It was these or naked." Kresley said.

"You look exhausted. There's a bed in my office upstairs," Shelby offered.

Kresley found it odd that the woman would have a bed in her office and it must have shown on her face because Shelby qualified, "Sometimes I bring my kids into work when we're between nannies and my husband is out on a case."

"A case?"

"He's with Alcohol, Tobacco, Firearms and Explosives. Dylan doesn't work regular hours."

Great the ATF and the FBI. No memory, but apparently Kresley was making herself known to every law-enforcement agency in existence. "How many children do you have?"

"Three," Shelby said with unfettered joy in her voice.

"Time for another one," came a voice from the direction of the stairway.

Suddenly a woman with bleached platinum hair appeared. She was a tribute to the eighties. Big hair, animal-print leggings, wide leather belt and mules with three-inch heels. Class and polish tempered by loud and gaudy.

Her green eyes fixed on Kresley like lasers. "So you're the one Matt fished out of the ocean who claims to have no memory?" Rose asked with skepticism.

Intimidated by the larger than life woman, Kresley just nodded.

Rose shook her head. "Well, if you ask me, you should be at a hospital getting medical care. What was Matt thinking?" The question was directed at Shelby.

"That there's no reason she should be in the hospital," Shelby said. "She'll have a good lunch and then Matt is going to take her home. Rose," Shelby continued, "I've spoken with Kendall and she assured me the memory loss is real. Trauma-induced amnesia."

Rose snorted. "I love my niece, but Kendall can be out there."

Kresley wondered if Rose ever looked in a mirror. She wasn't exactly a conformist.

"Don't forget, Kendall swears she met her husband in a past life. Nutty if you ask me."

"No one asked," Shelby said pointedly.

Matt appeared then, carrying a plate of food. Kresley was surprisingly glad to see him. Though Shelby had been warm, Rose was making her feel unwelcome. He placed the plate and a set of utensils on the bar. Kresley could feel the heat radiating off his body. She looked up, hoping to get a read on him but then she realized his entire attention was focused on Shelby. And then it hit her. "You're related," Kresley said, wagging her forefinger between Matt and Shelby.

"Ah-ha!" Rose clapped her hands once sharply. "See, it isn't just me. She thinks so, too," Rose said, the harshness gone from her tone. "I noticed it the moment he walked in here."

Matt looked at Kresley, though his eyes never really connected with hers. "We aren't related."

Rose made a 'Harrumph' sound, then turned, mumbling, and went back up the stairs.

"She's formidable," Kresley said as she poked at the tuna salad.

"She's all bark and no bite," Shelby assured her. "You just have to ease into Rose."

Kresley looked at Matt. "She wasn't very warm to you. How long did you say you'd been tending bar here?"

"A few weeks. By the way, I'm scheduled to work lunch," he said to Shelby.

"I'll call Susan in to cover for you."

"Thanks," he said, bending down only slightly to place a kiss against Shelby's cheek as she readied to leave the room.

In record speed, Kresley wolfed down the tuna salad, thanked everyone profusely, and then hurried out the back with Matt on her heels.

"What's the deal?" he asked.

"Lycra Lady hated me," she said.

Matt grinned. The action caused sexy dimples to appear on his cheeks. "Rose is just…*blunt*."

Kresley gingerly maneuvered herself into the passenger's seat. The lidocaine had worn off and she was starting to feel the pain of her injuries. "Who exactly got you my address?"

"Gabe got it off your DMV records."

Good God, *another* name to remember. "And Gabe is…?"

"Gabe Langston is a local P.I. and a friend. We met a few years back when Gabe came to Quantico for some training."

Kresley closed her eyes and relaxed against the headrest. Other than the single flash of a porthole, nothing else had sparked a memory. They crossed over Charleston Harbor and Sullivan's Island. Kresley knew that because she could read the road signs. At least she knew she could read. When Matt slowed and turned into a parking lot, there was nothing familiar about the apartment building at the corner of Hartnett Boulevard and Twenty-fifth Avenue. "I live here?"

"Unit 1B."

Matt pulled into a parking spot in front of the apartment. Kresley felt a tickle of uneasiness when she saw the door but nothing felt familiar.

"I'll go in with you."

Unlatching her seatbelt, she said, "Thank you."

They had barely stepped out of the car when a rotund woman with hair dyed a shade of red not known in nature hurried toward Kresley. Matt waited at a distance.

"You were supposed to come to the office two days ago," she said, her eyes little more than angry green slits.

"Because?" Kresley prompted.

"Because?" she spat. "You're three months behind on your share of the rent. You promised me you'd have the money to me yesterday. Instead you stayed out all night and half the day today." The woman was so worked up she punctuated her tirade by shaking her finger in Kresley's face. "Your roommate paid up. I want your share in a money order. No more rubber checks. Got it?"

Roommate? Kresley tried to hide her confusion. "Uh, how much do I owe you exactly?"

"Fifteen hundred plus another seventy-five in late fees."

"I seem to have lost my keys," Kresley said.

The landlady didn't appear to be the least bit sympathetic. Digging into the pocket of her housecoat, she yanked out a large ring, flipped through the keys, then removed one and handed it to Kresley. "Add another fifteen on for key replacement."

Matt waited until she'd waddled three or four feet back toward the door bearing a bronze plaque announcing Leasing Office before he joined Kresley. "She's a little ray of sunshine, isn't she?"

Kresley unlocked the door to unit 1B and opened it just a crack. Tilting her head back to compensate for his height, she said, "Well, thank you," and stuck out her right hand.

Matt chuckled softly. "That was a great kiss-off but if it's all the same to you, I'd like to take a look around, just to make sure the apartment is secure."

Matt came in and the first thing he noticed was a framed photograph of two women on a beach. One was Kresley.

The other one was Janice.

Chapter Three

As Kresley was looking around to see if any of these supposed roommates were home, Matt marched in like some recruit, his attention honed on a photograph on the entertainment center. There was no question. It was Janice. Turning the photo toward Kresley, he asked, "Who is this?"

As soon as she saw the image, she heard the words in her head again. *Trust no one*. "I—I don't know."

"Her name is Janice Cross," Matt said.

Kresley shook her head.

He reached her in three long strides. His blue eyes blazed as his fingers closed around her upper arms. "Think! She's six feet tall, has short brown hair."

"I know her," Kresley managed. "I don't know *how* I know her. Or *why*."

"That isn't very helpful," Matt said, scowling.

"I'm doing my best here," she shot back. "Kendall said my memory would come back in fits and starts so you'll just have to wait until I have the right fit or the right start. Now, thank you for everything you've done." She went to the door and opened it. "I need to shower and try to figure out where my bank is so I can see if I have enough money in my account to hopefully pay the mean landlady. So, good bye."

Grudgingly, Matt left.

Kresley was glad to be finally alone. She went to the kitchen first, opening the refrigerator to find only a jar of mustard surrounded by a half-dozen Chinese take-out cartons. There were several magnets on the fridge, all for restaurants that delivered.

The dishes in the dishwasher were clean and the place was tidy. She went down the hallway and found the first bedroom. In one bedroom, she picked a pair of size-ten panties off the floor. No way they belonged to her. Going to the closet, she found half the clothes were size ten; the others were a size six. Several gowns hung in the back, all with the expensive, exclusive label, Gianni.

Going to the second bedroom, she picked up a pillow and sniffed the faint scent of perfume. That didn't send a cascade of memories flooding back, either. She was so frustrated. Clearly there were other women sharing the apartment with her. If just one of her roommates came back, she could maybe get some answers to her questions. Opening the closet in this room revealed size twos and size fours. The size-two slacks were too long to be Kresley's, and, like the other closet, there were several Gianni gowns—these were a size two.

Of all the clothing, the size fours were the most

conservative and the most casual. The kind of thing you'd expect a graduate student to wear. *Like me?*

She decided this must be her bedroom. One she shared with a size two woman. All she saw was white furniture and girl stuff. Lots of pink things. Lots of lime green. A treadmill sat in the corner. Instead of its intended use, it was covered with blouses, dresses and slacks waiting to be ironed. There was a weight set as well as a kickboxing book on one side of the room. Kresley checked the treadmill clothes. Size two. By default, that made Kresley the kickboxer. There was a message board on the back of the door, but it had been wiped clean, leaving only hints of what had been written there. Two words, one started with the letter *O* maybe? Or *D?* Then what looked like a phone number since there were ten numbers beneath the top line. Too faint to make out.

Her search of the living room, dining room and computer nook also yielded nothing unique or special. It was a nice apartment. The only thing that was missing were her roommates. Her first instinct was to call and report them missing, but she didn't really know if they were missing. They could be on vacation, out shopping, spending the day at the beach—anything was possible. But the prickling sensation on the back of her neck told her something was wrong. Terribly wrong.

Then she realized what was missing. There wasn't much in the way of personal items. No credit cards, no driver's licenses, no catalogs, no junk mail. And no telephone. Not a single landline.

"Maybe we all used cell phones," Kresley said aloud. She added that to her list of things she needed to figure out.

There was a laptop in the small alcove. She powered it on and it asked for a password. Kresley's frustration level went up several notches. If it was her computer—which was only twenty-five percent possible—then the password was probably something she'd remember easily, like her birth date. Except right this instant, she didn't remember squat.

She cursed softly, then walked down to the leasing office. It wasn't that she wanted a bonus interaction with the landlady, she just needed to borrow a phone.

It took some doing, begging actually, and giving her the lone gold earring as collateral, to get the woman to loan Kresley her cell phone. Going back to her apartment, she had the weird feeling of being watched. Glancing around, she noticed nothing out of the ordinary and berated herself for being a wuss. Kresley called information for a number and then waited as the call was automatically dialed.

"Gabe Langston."

"Mr. Langston, we haven't met but my name is Kresley Hayes."

"How are you feeling?"

"A little disoriented. I was wondering if you could find out if I had a cell phone and if so, who the carrier is. Oh, and you don't happen to remember my birthday, do you?"

"April thirtieth," he said without missing a beat. "You'll be thirty at the end of the month."

"Good for me," adding that to her list of less-than-pleasant things. "My bank info?"

"Don't worry, turning thirty doesn't hurt as much as being shot."

"Well, that's something."

"Is my guy there?"

"Excuse me?"

"Don't get worried if you see a large blond guy with a neck like a redwood. He works for me."

"Why would I see him?"

"He's going to be watching out for you."

"I don't understand."

"Someone attacked you with a knife, then shot you and then tossed you in the Atlantic to drown. Matt and I agree that this person probably assumes you're dead, but just in case, Matt asked me to have someone keep an eye on you."

A chill danced along her spine. "I think my roommates are missing."

"When were they last seen?" Gabe asked.

"I'll find out from my landlady when I return her phone."

"Do that and then give me a call. In the meantime, I'll work on that bank information."

"Okay. Thanks." She clicked off, and headed for the bathroom to finally shower.

Very careful not to get her bandages wet—not an easy task by the way—Kresley enjoyed the feeling of the water pouring down on her. She was salty, sandy and sticky. And scared. The salt and sand washed off. The scared did not.

Knowing her name didn't mean she knew who she was. But at least it had given her something to focus on other than what might have happened out in the ocean. Though she was grateful to Matt and Gabe for their protection, she wondered if it was enough.

Going into the living room, she picked up the photo of Janice and herself at the beach. It was fairly recent; her own hair was the same length. Carefully, she slipped the photo out of the frame and stuck between the photo and the cardboard backing was a small slip of paper with a phone number.

She stopped toweling her hair dry and dialed the number. It rang six times, then went to voice mail. Unfortunately it was one of those pre-recorded voicemail announcements and not personalized. "Hi, this—" she started, then snapped the phone shut. What if the number belonged to whomever it was who'd tried to kill her? Maybe he wouldn't recognize her voice in the two syllables.

"Maybe you need to get a grip," Kresley told herself as she went around the apartment checking every lock.

She dried her hair, applied some makeup and managed to contort enough to dress in a green sleeveless, ruffled-neck blouse and white capris. Going back to the computer, she entered her birth date as a possible password. She was rewarded with a bright red error screen. Kresley tried her birth date backward. Another red error screen. Then just for the heck of it, she tried the ten digits she'd found hidden beneath the frame. Bingo she was in. Sort of.

There were several file folders in the computer, and many of those led to subfolders. The Gianni folder was the only name she recognized. The main folder contained five subfolders. Janice, Emma, Paula, Abby and Kresley. Unfortunately, no matter what she tried, the computer wouldn't let her open any of the files.

Giving up, she went to the Internet and typed in the telephone number that had gotten her into the computer. It wasn't listed on any of the public sites. Then she searched for herself and found her cell phone number. Writing it on a small piece of paper, she hit the redial number on the phone and again had it automatically connect her with Gabe Langston.

"Langston."

"Hi, it's Kresley. Any luck finding my bank or cell company?"

He rattled off account numbers and the names and addresses of the closest branches and stores. "You own a lime-green VW Beetle," he added. "Is it there?"

Kresley peeked out of the drawn drapes. "No."

"I'll have someone check the parking lot at the docks."

"I've found a phone number and some names. Is there any way—"

"Read them off."

Kresley did as he asked and in a matter of seconds, he had the names of her roommates. Emma Rooper, Abby Howell and Janice Cross. Only Paula remained unidentified.

"That's interesting."

"What?"

"Janice Cross. That's the woman in the photo that Matt was so interested in learning more about."

KRESLEY FIGURED her landlady would be a lot more accommodating if she showed up with the back rent. She was glad Gabe had warned her about her thick-necked shadow because he stuck to her like glue as she walked the block and a half to her bank.

She was a lefty with a bandaged left hand and unfortunately the withdrawal slip required her signature. If they asked for ID, she was toast. If she had to guess, her identification was somewhere at the bottom of the Atlantic. The best she could muster was an old expired driver's license she'd found in her panty drawer.

A thin sheen of perspiration covered her as she waited in the orderly line, created by burgundy velvet ropes. The entire time, she prayed silently. Prayed that she had enough money. Prayed that she wouldn't get snagged by lack of identification.

A year later—okay, it just felt that long—Kresley stepped up to the available teller. "Hi, I'm—"

"Kresley! What happened to your hand?" the young brunette woman with the cheery smile asked.

"Um, accident with a knife," she said as she slid the withdrawal slip across the veneered counter.

"You should be more careful...."

Kresley tuned her out, not to be rude but because she was relieved at not being interrogated. She'd been so terrified of not being able to answer questions, she'd actually written her address and birth date on the palm of her good hand.

"Here you go," the teller said with a wave and a broad grin. "One money order, a receipt and a hundred dollars." The teller set them out as if dealing a hand of cards.

"Thank you," Kresley said, sticking it all inside her empty purse and stepping away from the window.

Her next stop was the phone store where she bought a cell phone. Then, as the sun was setting, she walked the short distance back to her apartment complex, in search of her landlady. She knocked on the door and the landlady yelled to come in. She'd supplemented her central air conditioning with a large window unit that made a strained rattling sound. Her apartment was the same floor plan as Kresley's, though instead of a living room, she had it set up as an office.

"What now?"

"I brought back your phone and I want to clear up my back rent." She reached into her purse and handed over the money order.

Scowling, the woman pursed lips that were poorly outlined in an unnatural orange-brown. "I've been hounding you for months. How come you can pay now?"

"Does it matter?" Kresley asked.

The woman shrugged and her dull brown eyes narrowed. "Need something else?"

"I want a copy of the rental agreement and background checks on me and my roommates if possible."

"Sure," the landlady shrugged and rolled a cheap office chair over to the filing cabinets and took out a file marked 1B. She rolled over to a copy machine, managing to do everything without ever leaving her chair. Kresley thanked her.

Her response was, "Yeah, well, just remember next month's rent is due in sixteen days."

Returning to her apartment, Kresley heard a car pulling into the lot. The sound spooked her, so she jerked her head to see if it was her thick-necked bodyguard.

It was Matt's Jeep.

"Before you get mad," he began before he even cut the engine. "I'm here on Kendall's orders. She said with the concussion someone should check on you. I'm just—" Matt stopped in mid-sentence to answer his cell. "DeMarco."

"It's Gabe. The Coast Guard just found the *Carolina Moon*."

"And?"

"Lots of blood and lots of bodies."

"Janice?"

"Sorry, all I got from my contact was two female victims and three male victims."

Chapter Four

He probably should have told Kresley that the yacht had been found, but since he didn't know her involvement or lack thereof, it seemed prudent to keep her out of the loop.

Finding the rental applications on the coffee table was something of a bonanza. He'd been fully prepared to show his badge and get them from the landlady, however, Kresley had apparently saved him the trouble. This whole thing had already blossomed out of control and he needed to get a grip on it before it got any worse.

Since it would take at least four hours for the Coast Guard to tow the *Carolina Moon* into port and then process the scene, Matt sat on Kresley's sofa until she fell asleep. Before he left for the dock to see what he could find out, Matt took Kresley's cell to make a clone of it. Not ethical but it was for her safety, and might help him get a solid lead on Janice, and what she was involved in.

Then he went over to the laptop, tapped the touchpad and brought it to life. He logged into the FBI database. Emma Rooper and Abby Howell appeared to be normal young women. Abby was a waitress at a restaurant called The Grille in Summerville. Emma worked for a pawn shop. He accessed their tax returns and found that in the past three years, neither of the women had made more than twenty grand. Matt typed in Kresley's information.

Eyes Only.

"What the hell?" Matt said, reentering his password and again attempting to access her file. Same result.

Sitting back in the chair, he raked his fingers through his hair trying to figure out why a grad student in South Carolina would have an Eyes Only FBI file.

Using his cell phone, he called Gabe. "Can you check to see the last time Kresley's phone was used?" Matt asked, then gave him the number.

"Day before yesterday at 7:20 p.m."

"What number was called?" Matt asked.

Gabe read it off, then had Matt hold while he called it. "Nothing. My guess is it's a prepaid. It's going straight to voice mail."

"I'll swing by and get you," Matt said.

He checked on Kresley. She was fast asleep and his sympathies went out to her. He was fairly certain sure that she was hip-deep—whether she knew it or not—in whatever Janice was up to now.

The only illumination in the room was a small sliver of moonlight slicing through the room. It gave

Kresley's pretty face a soft glow. Absently, he reached out and tucked a strand of hair behind her ear, then he left to meet up with Gabe and get an up-close look at the 135-foot yacht, the *Carolina Moon.*

"Do you know any more yet?" Matt asked as Gabe squeezed his six-foot-four-inch frame into the passenger's seat of the Jeep.

Gabe shook her head.

The short ride felt like it took forever. Matt steeled himself, half expecting to find Janice zipped into one of the body bags.

"What took them so long to bring the yacht in?" Matt asked.

"It drifted into international waters. Usual governmental jurisdictional bullshit. Present company excepted."

If Janice wasn't on the boat, then where was she? What had happened? The only person who could answer that, he suspected, was Kresley. Even though he felt a clock ticking away the minutes, he had to wait out her trauma-induced amnesia.

When they reached the dock, banks of high-power floodlights shone down on every nook and cranny. The yacht was a Heesen—worth from eight to eighty million, depending on the accessories. Matt parked and, thanks to Gabe's friendship with Gary Ross, one of the detectives, they were welcomed beneath the yellow crime-scene tape at the end of the dock.

He was a good ten feet from the boat but Matt could easily see the blood on the deck, splattered everywhere. It even ran down the sides of the white hull.

The medical examiner's minions were unzipping five body bags. Gabe quietly said something to Detective Ross, then they were given paper booties and allowed aboard. Ross came over to Matt and asked, "Is this the woman you think was on the boat?"

He shook his head. "That's not Janice."

Ross led him to the second corpse. "How about her?"

"No. Not her, either." Matt felt a weight lift off his shoulders.

"Recognize this?" Ross asked, holding a small sealed bag with a single earring in it.

He recognized it all right. It belonged to Kresley. She'd been wearing its mate when he found her.

Matt was trying to find a way to equivocate without actually lying outright when Gabe spoke up.

"You IDed the men?" Gabe asked, steering the detective toward the male victims.

Ross nodded. "That one," he said pointing to the one being lifted to a gurney, "according to his driver's license, is Thomas Gibson, Jr. The other one is Jason Wellington, Jr."

"They had their identification on them?" Matt asked.

Ross nodded. "Oddly, neither of the women had purses. The guys were in tuxes and the women in fancy gowns, but they had no purses. Hell, my wife won't drive to the corner store without a purse."

"What about the captain—?"

"Found his body below deck. Wasn't sliced and diced like the other four. Shot."

"With a .22?" Matt asked.

"You psychic or do you have something you'd like to share with the class?"

"Just a guess," Matt shrugged. Had the captain been shot with the same weapon used on Kresley? "Have you found the gun?"

"Not the gun. Not the knife," the detective replied.

Matt strolled carefully along the edge of the yacht, taking care not to disturb the blood. "The dinghy is still tied up."

Gabe and the detective came up beside him. "So, unless the purses and weapons helped each other off the boat, they had company."

"Did you dust the ladder?" Matt asked.

"Lots of smudges and a partial. Small, either a man's pinkie finger or could be a woman's print."

"Have they been run yet?" Matt asked.

"Not yet," Ross said. "Once we finish processing the scene, then we'll start scanning the prints through the system."

Gabe patted Ross on the back. "Sounds like you've got it all covered."

"Naw, too much blood," Ross countered. "And the galley is stocked for eight dinner guests. I think what we're looking at is half a crime scene."

SO FOUR OF the dinner guests were missing. This fact gave Matt a glimmer of hope. Especially after he saw the smudge of red paint along the port side of the yacht. Now all he needed to do was find a red boat that might have been tied up to the yacht—one of whose occupants may have been Janice. Only problem? Too many maybes and assumptions. Truth be told, there was a greater possibility that Janice had been killed and her body tossed into the ocean.

Near dawn he headed back to Kresley. He knocked on the door of possibly the only person with answers to what had gone down on the yacht—if she could only remember them.

IT HAD BEEN more than twenty-four hours since Matt had pulled her out of the ocean and what had Kresley learned? That she was a left-handed woman who was behind on her rent, even though she had sufficient funds in her bank account to make the fifteen-hundred-dollar payment. Oh, and the gown. "Let's not forget the gown," she muttered as she got up on tiptoes and peered through the peephole.

"Good morning," she said, opening the door just enough so that turned sideways, she was blocking his path.

"Smells like you made muffins," he said with a smile that reached all the way to his eyes.

She couldn't help but smile back. "One-handed, no less."

"Do I get one? I did save your life."

Kresley tilted her head to one side. "You know this isn't *I Dream of Jeannie*. I'm not going to do your bidding for the rest of my life."

"I am not feeling the gratitude."

"If I give you a muffin, will you go away?"

"Maybe. Why, you have a big day planned?"

He followed her inside and couldn't resist asking, "Any more memories or flashes?"

She shook her head. "Sorry," she said as she took a lemon-and-poppy-seed muffin off a plate and handed it to him.

"Then why so chipper?" He shoved his hands into the front pockets of his shorts.

She turned, her blue eyes sparkling with amusement. "Having Thor helps," she admitted.

"Thor?"

"My bodyguard. Since he won't agree to coming in for food or to use the facilities, I baked him some muffins and refilled his thermos."

Matt felt his brows knit together. "That's it?"

"And I found this," she said, moving into the living room, holding her bandaged hand up.

She was probably in pain and just as probably not the type to whine about it. He wasn't sure if he respected that or wanted her lying in bed with her injured hand on a soft pillow. Kresley and bed in the same thought was a mistake. *Huge mistake*.

She had a fairly athletic shape, taut and toned, but all that got lost when someone, hell, someone like *him,* got a look at the generous outline of her breasts. He pinched his eyes shut for a half second. It wasn't as if Kresley Hayes was the first, nor would she be the last attractive blonde with flawless skin who left a scent like a vapor trail in her wake. A good smell—a dab of some sort of floral perfume that didn't completely obscure the unique and seductive odor he could smell practically a mile away.

"I have something great to show you."

Matt swallowed the guilt generated by his wayward thoughts, nearly choking in the process.

Sitting down on the couch, she patted the spot next to her. Matt obliged, all the while reminding his body that his brain and not parts farther south were running this operation.

Reaching under the coffee table, she pulled out a photo album and some files. Opening the album, she tapped her fingertip on the page of photographs mounted beneath yellowing film. "This has to be me," she said, excitedly. "See the small mole just under my left eye?"

"Yes."

"It matches this one," she told him, touching her cheek. She flipped each page, stopping for a few seconds for him to see the pictures.

It was Kresley at the beach. Playing in the snow. Opening Christmas gifts. Pretty much every milestone from infancy through her freshman year at college.

Then it ended abruptly. "That's a nice album," he remarked.

"It is," she agreed on a quick rush of breath. "It also answered a lot of questions for me. I was an only child."

He nodded. "Or maybe you were just prettier than your siblings."

She gave him a little sarcastic smile. "See this photograph of me and my parents under the Welcome Freshmen sign?"

He nodded.

"Well, I took a magnifying glass and if you look out this window next to my father, you'll see the College of Charleston logo."

Matt lifted the album and focused on the small sign barely visible in the image. "Okay."

"I called the bursar's office, then they transferred me to the admissions office and eventually I learned I got my undergraduate degree three years ago. And I've finished the first three quarters of my Master's degree."

He didn't have the heart to tell her that he already knew all of that. She seemed so proud of herself. She was smiling and he saw no reason to rain on her parade.

"I checked and when I entered as a freshman, I had a Maryland address and my parents' names were Gregory and Evelyn. I was just about to go online and see if I could track down—"

Matt reached over and tucked some loose strands of hair behind her ear. "Kresley, you've got—"

"Parents," she said eagerly. "If I talk to them, I'm sure to remember more."

Matt shook his head, then met her gaze. "Your parents died seven years ago." He rested his palm against her cheek. "That's why the photo album ends when it does."

She pushed his hand away and stood up. She paced between the entertainment center and the arm of the sofa. Without missing a step, she asked, "You already knew about my parents, didn't you?"

"Yes."

"When?"

"It doesn't matter," he said, standing and moving so that she had no choice but to stop pacing or plow into him.

"It matters to me."

"I ran a background check on you once your prints were identified."

She tilted her head back, her eyes blinking against the threat of tears. "That was more than a day ago. Why keep it a secret?"

"Doctor's orders."

"What?"

"Kendall said you'd already suffered enough emotional trauma and that I shouldn't do anything to make it worse."

"Honesty doesn't make anything worse. Secrets do. What else do you know about me?" she demanded, one hand on her hip and a stern glint in her eyes.

"Your parents died in a car accident on their drive back from dropping you off at college. I'm sorry," he said softly.

She gazed down at the worn Berber carpet. "I don't remember them."

The pain and emptiness in her tone stabbed him in the gut. Matt reached out and drew her into his arms. He stroked her hair as he felt her silent tears dampen his shirt. She stayed in his embrace for a few minutes, then stepped back.

Wiping away her tears with the back of her hand, she asked, "What else?" Her eyes scanned his face. "What. Else?"

Blowing out a breath, he replied, "No siblings. Your parents left enough money for you to graduate from college, but that was it. You went to work. You started a relationship with another teacher at the school. After a year you were engaged."

Kresley looked down at her left hand. No ring. "Who am I engaged to?" she asked.

"No one. You broke it off three weeks before the wedding."

"Why?"

"It doesn't matter."

"It does to me," she said. "You've got details about my life. I don't have anything. I was actually happy this morning that I remembered how to make muffins. Happy! Forty-eight hours ago I was shot and stabbed and making freaking muffins made me happy. Do you have any idea how lame that is? I don't remember parents who obviously loved me. I don't remember being engaged. Stop trying to protect me and tell me what you know."

"The guy's name was David Avery."

"Why did I cancel the wedding?"

"Mr. Avery was having an affair with your maid of honor."

"Not much of an endorsement for my ability to read people, is it?"

"Paula and David were very discreet."

She scoffed and shook her head. "How discreet did they have to be?"

Matt winced. "Very. Until a month ago, Paula was your roommate."

She laughed without humor. "At least my fiancé didn't have to go far to cheat." Kresley pressed the heel of her unbandaged hand against her forehead. "Next thing you're going to tell me is that they are responsible for whatever happened to me."

"No," Matt assured her. "David and Paula moved out of state. They haven't been in South Carolina since the breakup. Their alibi is solid."

She took in a deep breath and released it slowly. "I had a cheating fiancé and a lying maid of honor but they weren't the ones who hurt me…now, so who did? Was it one of my roommates?"

"Sit down," Matt said, bracketing her shoulders as she veered around the coffee table. "You haven't remembered anything about them, have you?"

"No. But I got their names from Gabe and one of them," she paused and went through the files she'd gotten from her landlady. "This one. Janice Cross. Isn't that the woman you were asking me about? The one in that photo?" She pointed to the entertainment center.

Matt nodded.

"Are the two of you—"

"We're partners," Matt clarified before she could even finish the thought. "She boarded the *Carolina Moon* two nights ago."

"And you think I was on that boat?"

"I know you were," Matt said. "Unless your earring went all by itself."

"Why would I be on it?"

"Don't know yet. Gabe and I went to the yacht last night," he said.

The color instantly drained from her face. "They found it?"

"Yep. Drifting offshore."

"How bad was it?"

"Bad," Matt said, "and it isn't going to take the cops long to match your fingerprints. They were planning on doing a full canvass of the dock area. Someone is bound either to give them your identity or come up with a pretty decent sketch. And they're probably going to find your car. It's parked in the lot with the date-and-time-stamped ticket between the dashboard and the windshield."

"Then I should call them and let them know I'm okay."

"If you want to get arrested, sure."

"Why would they arrest me? I have injuries that prove I was attacked."

"Or injuries that prove at least one of the victims fought back."

"So what do you suggest?"

"We help each other out."

"How?"

"You and Janice were on that yacht. Her body hasn't been recovered. I need to find her and it's possible that you were the last person to see her."

"Except I can't remember anything."

Matt hooked his finger beneath her chin, forcing her to meet his gaze. "Yet."

"Can you tell me about you and Janice?" Kresley asked. "Maybe that will jog my memory."

Matt took a deep breath, then began. "Janice and

I spent two years in New York working our way up the food chain of the Russian mafia. My cover was blown so we were pulled off the case." He leaned against the arm of the sofa. "The Russians make the Italians and the Colombians look like Rotarians. They've got tentacles in everything—drugs, weapons, counterfeiting. And they'll kill anyone who gets in their way. The remnants of the slaughter I saw on the yacht had all the hallmarks of a Russian mob hit.

"If they had found out Janice was a federal agent, believe me, they would have made sure her remains were prominently displayed on the yacht. Since there was no sign of her, I have to believe she somehow escaped the massacre."

"So why isn't the whole FBI here looking for her?"

Matt raked his fingers through his hair.

"Janice hasn't been following protocols and I've been filing bogus status reports so the bureau chief wouldn't catch on. So I could lose my job, along with Janice. That's why I can't contact the bureau about her disappearance. Not until I learn more. I can't risk outing her and possibly breaching her cover. That could get her killed. If she is still alive, that is."

"Since she was your partner, can't you look into her cases and figure out which one this might be related to?"

"The last case she was working on was the Russian mob. When that soured, she got a lead on a drug-smuggling ring working out of Charleston that looked to have ties in the Russian mob. If she could make the link, the Russian case could be made. Then three months ago she went off the grid completely. And I've been covering her tail since."

"Isn't that going a little above and beyond?" Kresley asked.

"It wasn't the smartest decision I've ever made, but Janice did me a huge favor."

"What was the favor?"

"She found out I lied on my FBI application and didn't reveal that to my superiors."

Chapter Five

"What was the lie?" Kresley asked softly.

Matt hesitated for a moment, then blurted out, "I knew that my biological father Ned Nichols was a felon. Lying about it is grounds for immediate dismissal."

Kresley was silent for a moment, and then reached out and gently squeezed Matt's forearm.

"There's more," he said, grimacing. "Shelby Tanner is my half sister. Ned is her father, too. When I was a teenager, visiting my maternal grandmother, she told me about Shelby. I honestly didn't give her a thought until Janice, who had just come to Charleston, called me in New York. She'd gone to the Rose Tattoo, and was struck immediately by Shelby's resemblance to me. Knowing my history, she sent me some photos. The minute I saw Shelby I knew she was my sister. I hired Gabe to check Shelby out."

"But they seem so friendly. He agreed to spy on a friend?"

"Yeah, well, that was the problem. Next thing I

know he's at my office in New York trying to figure out what kind of threat I am to Shelby and her family."

"Good for him."

"Anyway, we went out, had some drinks, and the next thing Gabe's arranging for me to work at the Rose Tattoo so Shelby and I can get to know each other before I spring this on her."

"She seems to like you well enough, so what are you waiting for?"

"I did the math. I'm only three months older than Shelby. She might not like learning that her father was fooling around with my mother while he was married to hers. Then there's the felon thing. And if she finds out the truth, all she has to do is make one phone call to the FBI and my career is toast."

"I think you should just talk to her. She seems really nice."

"In two weeks I won't have a choice."

"Why?"

"Shelby's husband Dylan will inform her if I don't. Gabe strongly suggested I tell her first."

His hesitation had been stupid, but not without motivation. After his mother died, he'd spent his childhood bouncing from one foster home to the next. Setting himself up for rejection wasn't something he did easily. But Dylan had given him a time frame. Hell, it had taken Matt a ton of negotiation just to get the other man to agree to keep his identity a secret from his wife. Apparently, Dylan and Shelby didn't have secrets.

Not like the load threatening to bury him. He wanted to punch something. Mostly himself. What a convoluted mess he'd made of things. He should have told Shelby already. He should have shut Janice down. The consequences of not doing that was that civilians, like Kresley, were stuck dead center.

AT MIDDAY, Matt pulled into a parking spot behind the Rose Tattoo. It was Sunday, notoriously slow, but after church service would start in about an hour and realizing he'd miss the shift, he needed to inform Rose and Shelby that he wouldn't make it.

As before Matt led Kresley through the kitchen to the bar, then left her testing her cell's features and sipping a tall glass of sweet tea.

He wasn't sure why he'd shared his secret with Kresley. Going up the narrow stairs to the second floor, he wondered how many other people would find out before he told the one person who really mattered. Shelby.

Knocking twice, he stood in the open doorway as Shelby looked up from the spreadsheet in the center of her tidy desk. She was thirty-four years old, raven-haired, with bright-blue eyes and an oval face. Even after giving birth to three children, she was trim and fit. She carried herself with confidence and greeted everyone with a warm smile.

Matt was no exception.

"Come in," she said. "How many times do I have to tell you that if the door's open, just walk in?"

"I have a favor to ask," Matt began, his gaze

floating around the room taking in the framed photographs and the artwork of her children taped to the walls. Most of it was Chad's, her oldest child who'd just started kindergarten. Cassidy had been born nine months after Shelby had married Dylan, followed quickly by Carly, who was just shy of her first birthday. Hard to fathom that these kids were family to him.

Matt always felt odd in Shelby's office. Not just because of his secret, either. Shelby's office was all done in frou-frou antiques that didn't look sturdy enough to hold his weight. Her desk and everything else was mahogany with silk-covered cushions and narrow legs. Matt cringed when the seat creaked under his weight.

"What can I do for you?"

"I need a little emergency time off."

"Is everything okay?" Shelby asked.

"That woman I fished out of the ocean yesterday morning..."

Shelby nodded. "Yes?"

"She still has some health problems and no family and—"

Shelby held her hand up. "I understand. I think it's very nice of you to help a total stranger."

"Thanks," Matt said, grateful and guilty all at once. He'd told Gabe. Then Dylan. Then Kresley. He needed to work up the nerve to tell Shelby the truth.

Shelby stood up. Even in flat shoes, she was nearly as tall as Matt. She walked past him, leading the way to the office next door.

Unlike Shelby's ultrafeminine office, Rose's office reflected her obsession. Every inch had some sort of tribute to Elvis. Elvis paintings, Elvis statues, Elvis bobbleheads. Name it and Rose had it. According to Susan Taylor, the restaurant manager, Rose's apartment was all things Elvis, as well.

Rose greeted Shelby with a smile. Matt received a glare. "What's up?"

"Matt's going to take a little time off. I don't have a problem with that, do you?"

Rose asked, "Why?"

Again, Matt explained about Kresley's memory problem and her lack of family and played up the helplessness aspect. Though the way she'd tossed him on his butt when he'd first found him made him think *helpless* was not one of Kresley's personality traits.

"Go ahead," Rose said, sounding more put out than she looked.

He thanked them both, then started back downstairs. When he reached the bottom, a tall woman sporting a magenta mohawk and no fewer than eight piercings he could see greeted him. There were more, he knew, but they were hidden beneath her clothing. She'd offered to show them to him on a few occasions. Not in a sexual way, she was just proud of her body bling.

"Hey," Susan said in a slow, southern drawl. "Met your girlfriend. Not much on chitchat, is she?"

"She's not my girlfriend," Matt said quickly. Maybe too quickly. "Mind keeping an eye on her for a few minutes?"

Susan gave him an odd look. "You want me to babysit a grown woman?"

"It's complicated," he said. "Just be nice to her while I run across the street to see Gabe, please? She could use a friend right about now."

Susan nodded. "I sensed that. Her aura is a livid light gray. That means her psyche is in a serious state of terror."

"Very insightful," Matt said, tolerating Susan's New Age leanings.

"I could do a crystal cleansing," she said, her tone growing excited at the prospect. "Or better still, take her to my friend Selma. Her spells always work."

"I'll get back to you on that," Matt said. "Choosing between crystals and a Wiccan spell isn't a decision to be made lightly."

Susan smiled. "You're right. If you can't choose, I could always do a tarot reading. Wait a sec," Susan added, her contact-lens-tinted violet eyes shining with excitement. "I've got an amulet and some lemon oil in my car. Aromatherapy might help until you decide."

Matt smiled indulgently. Susan was as kind and well-intentioned as she was loony.

"Don't worry," Susan said. "I'll make sure she's comfy while you do…whatever."

KRESLEY DIDN'T KNOW what to say as the woman with the spiky purple hair slipped the necklace over her head. A bottle in the shape of a teardrop hung on the chain, and the scent of citrus was almost overpowering. "Thank you," Kresley said.

"I'm already seeing a change in your aura," she said, standing back. Like the other Rose Tattoo employees, she was dressed in a black oxford shirt and black pants. The only splash of color was the rose embroidered on the breast pocket. It matched the rose painted on the front bay window and repeated on the napkins and napkin rings.

"We open for lunch in a half hour, so I've got some things to do. Feel free to go behind the bar if you want more tea. Or fix yourself a *real* drink if you want."

Susan disappeared into the kitchen for a second, then returned with a small platter of appetizers.

"DeLancey sent these out for us to sample," Susan said. "The date thingy with the bacon is to die for."

Kresley popped one in her mouth. "That's amazing," she said, wiping her fingers on the beverage napkin. "If I worked in a place like this I'd probably weigh two hundred pounds."

"DeLancey is a great chef," Susan said after eating one of the crab puffs. "Has a great life, too. Husband who loves her. Kids. And she loves her job. She has a pristine aura."

"My aura must be awful," Kresley remarked as she selected another puff pastry.

"It is problematic," Susan agreed.

"So, what got you into auras?" Kresley asked.

Susan shrugged. "Now you sound like my father. He's waiting for me to come to my senses." The latter part of the sentence included air quotes. "I know people find me a little weird," Susan admitted.

"Okay, a *lot* weird. But I just haven't found anything that fits yet, know what I mean?"

Kresley laughed. "Very well. I went someplace almost two full days ago and all I know about myself is that I'm left-handed, have no living relatives, no cash but I somehow managed to wash ashore wearing a very expensive evening gown."

"What gown?" Susan asked from the opposite side of the bar where she was filling compartments with slices of lemons, limes and oranges.

"A Gianni gown."

Susan whistled. "I know people who'd give a kidney for a Gianni original."

"Maybe that's why I was behind on my rent. How much does a Gianni cost?"

Susan shrugged. "Three grand and up. Emphasis on the up."

"Does he use gold thread or something?"

"Actually, I think he has done. I read in the paper that he'd used real gold accent stitches for some debutante's dress a couple of years ago."

"I went from teaching to full-time graduate student. How could I possibly afford a pricey designer gown?"

"Why don't you go ask?" Susan suggested.

"Excuse me?"

"His salon opens at one on Sundays. Why not go ask the guy?"

"Go ask what guy?" Matt asked as he walked in from the kitchen.

"The gown," Kresley said. "Do you have it?"

"In the back of the Jeep."

"So," Kresley said as she slipped off the barstool. "Maybe he can explain how I paid for it."

Matt nodded. "It's worth a try."

"Which way?" Kresley asked Susan.

"Go out, make a left. Then go two blocks to Queen Street. Make another left and his place is on the right side of the street."

It was a warm, sunny day with nothing but fluffy white clouds and the sounds of gulls woven into the fabric of noonday traffic. Shielding her eyes from the bright sun, Kresley with Matt in tow followed a group of tourists turning a map counter-clockwise as they argued over the best way to reach Fort Sumter. "Shouldn't I get a driver's license and replace my credit cards?" she asked as they walked.

"Only if you want to advertise the fact that you're alive and well."

"Good point," she said, picking up the pace to compensate for his long strides.

The sun burned her shoulders and the air was thick, humid and slightly "off" smelling. A minute later, she heard the clip-clop of a hansom cab and realized the odor was horse manure. She looked down the block, eventually sighting a wooden sign on the opposite side of the street with the designer's name and logo sculpted into it.

Just as she was about to cross, Matt turned, smiling, then his expression suddenly changed.

Stopping in mid stride, Matt tackled her just as the glass window of the shop behind them exploded into shards.

The acrid smell of gunpowder would have choked her if she could breathe, which she couldn't. Not with Matt's body on top of her.

He rolled off her; his gun discreetly appeared in his right hand. Matt straddled her, making it impossible for Kresley to move. She heard the squeal of tires, though they sounded at least a block away.

Matt strung a few expletives together, as he helped her to her feet. "You okay?"

"Someone shot at us," she panted out, still shaking with terror.

"Are you hit?" he asked, running his hands from her head to her toes.

"No. Why would someone shoot at me in broad daylight? Forget that. Why shoot me at all?"

He returned the gun to the back of his waistband, the bulge hidden by his shirt.

"Should we call the police?"

Matt took her hand and hurried her across the street. "Not until we figure out who to trust."

Trust no one. The tall brunette's words echoed in her brain. She stopped nearly in the center of the street. "Your partner, Janice, told me not to trust anyone."

Matt practically pulled her off her feet. "Let's get into Gianni's and then we can talk, but not out in the open. That black SUV might turn around for a second pass."

She remained too frozen by fear to move.

"Let's go," Matt whispered close to her ear. His calm tone was soothing.

They raced across the street as the owner of the small T-shirt shop came out. His face registered shock as he surveyed the damage. The window was history and most of the clothing on display was covered in a sparkling dust of shattered glass. The shopkeeper looked to be in his mid-fifties. He was bald and his brown eyes were open wide as he tried to comprehend what had happened to his store.

"Even though the shooter used a silencer, it won't take the cops long to determine someone shot out that window." The sensation of his warm breath on her skin gave her goose bumps. So did the knowledge that someone had tried to kill her. Again. "Absolutely. I don't want to be here when the cops come," she said with conviction.

As they crossed the street to the designer dress shop, Matt said, "Just a few more feet, you can do it."

Matt placed his hand at the center of her back. His fingers splayed, sending heat radiating outward to all her nerve endings. Kresley's whole body was on fire by the time they reached the salon of Gianni. "She gave me—oops." Kresley lifted the chain around her neck. The teardrop amulet must have smashed when she hit the ground. Now she just had an oily stain on the front of her shirt. "I wonder what the metaphysical punishment is for breaking an amulet."

The shop was closed.

"Dammit," she muttered. Bracketing her face with her hands, she peered inside. No lamps were lit but there was sufficient daylight for her to see into the shop. There were three burgundy velvet sofas, a square center table and several smaller end tables, all with glass tops. At the far end of the showroom was a raised, circular stage with eight mirrored panels so a woman trying on a dress could see herself from every angle. There were curtains on either side of the stage, dark and heavy to match the material on the sofas.

"Look familiar?" Matt asked.

Closing her eyes, Kresley tried to conjure a memory associated with the salon. Nothing. Turning to glance up at him, she shook her head. "Nothing is familiar."

"We'll come back in the morning," Matt said as he took his cell phone out of his pocket.

While Kresley stood by feeling completely useless, he pressed a single button and said, "Hey, Gabe. I need a partial plate run. Black SUV—illegal tint on the windows, maybe an Escalade. First digits are eight-three-three."

As people passed by them, both on foot and in vehicles, Kresley saw danger everywhere. If someone looked at her for longer than a second, her stomach clenched. If someone slowed their car, even fractionally, her stomach clenched.

"Let's go someplace less public," Matt suggested. He looked down at her and frowned.

Wrapping his arms around her, he drew her against him. Settled against his hard, muscular body Kresley felt an instantaneous sense of relief. Matt's embrace assuaged her fears; she no longer thought of guns, knives and killers.

It did something else, too. Kresley could hear the soft rhythm of his heartbeat against her ear. Feel the staccato rise and fall of his chest with each breath. Smell the clean, slightly woodsy scent of soap.

Kresley summoned the strength to step out of his hold. He was looking at her with such compassion in those brilliant blue eyes that she almost threw herself back into the safety of his arms.

She heard the approach of sirens. "Guess we'd better go."

Matt took hold of her right hand and led her through an alley. They turned up Chalmers Street to Bay, ending up a short block from the Rose Tattoo. Kresley assumed they were headed back to the restaurant, but Matt led her behind the restaurant to an adjacent building.

Matt dropped her hand, dug into his pocket and pulled out a key ring. Inserting one of the three keys on it into the knob, he gave a turn and she heard the tumblers slide open.

"This is a nice place."

The apartment decor was…eclectic. They walked directly into the living room which had a functional couch covered in a different-shades-of-blue striped fabric. Judging by the wear patterns on the armrests, it had been around for a while. There was a small, laminate coffee table and a matching laminate entertainment center. There was a television set, a DVD player and a stack of DVDs. Tilting her head to the side, Kresley read a few of the titles, mostly horror and science fiction.

The living room gave way to a small, narrow galley kitchen with a refrigerator and stove.

"That's the bedroom," he said, pointing to one of three closed doors. "Middle is the bathroom."

She stepped around him and went to look at the bedroom. The bed was hastily made. Other than that, the room was tidy and cozy. Next, she inspected the bathroom. The minute she opened the door, she smelled it. A clean, woodsy scent. Matt.

On closer inspection, she saw a razor on the vanity along with a toothbrush holder with one toothbrush hanging in place. There was a half-used bar of soap in the dish and two sets of towels hung on the rod of the shower door. An organizer hung from the showerhead. Shampoo and another used bar of soap occupied the top shelf.

She turned and met Matt's gaze full-on. "You live here?"

"Yep. We should be safe here."

"I don't think this is a great idea. What if the person who shot at us comes here? I'd be putting you in serious danger."

"I'm a big boy and I'm a good shot. Don't worry," Matt replied with a disarming wink as punctuation. His cell then rang. "DeMarco," he said, one hand cupped as he moved toward the front door.

"It's Gabe. My source in the Coast Guard came through. Kresley is definitely involved in the yacht massacre and Janice's disappearance," Gabe said. "They found Janice's fingerprints on the *Carolina*

Moon. The female victims have been definitely identified as Abigail Howell and Emma Rooper."

"They're Kresley's missing roommates. Who identified them? Were their prints on file?"

"Nope," Gabe answered. "Their IDs were in their purses. Also recovered. So was Kresley's, by the way. All stashed in a bulkhead. Two sets of prints haven't yet been identified."

"Anything new on the two men?"

"A couple of investment counselors. Tom Gibson was the one who actually rented the yacht. Dinner cruise for eight," Gabe said.

Matt rubbed his chin wondering who might belong to the unidentified prints. "Any way to determine if Janice was on the yacht when the carnage happened?"

"Janice's prints were lifted from the area around the dive ladder. Kresley is another story. She left prints in the blood of the other victims. Whatever happened, she was in the thick of it."

"They scraped paint off the hull of the boat. The working theory is that a second boat was tied to the *Carolina Moon* and that's how the killer got away."

"Good theory. If there was a second boat, it would explain Janice's disappearance."

"The cops know Janice is FBI."

"You're sure?"

"Yes. And because of that, they are going to focus on Kresley. Are you absolutely positive she isn't the killer?"

"Positively. You haven't met her, but it would be

virtually impossible for a woman her size to have killed six or seven people. The wounds on her hands are defensive. My guess is she fought back, and then jumped into the water."

"Maybe Janice did the same thing," Gabe suggested.

"Possible. Since she's a champion swimmer, I'm having a hard time imagining that she's drowned.

"What can they do with the paint transfer?" Matt asked.

"Run lab tests but marine paint isn't as unique as automobile paint."

"Nothing unique about it?" Matt asked.

"It's the same color red the Coast Guard uses."

"That's not very helpful. Unless one of the Coast Guard boats scraped the yacht." Matt paused and rubbed his forehead. "I think we can assume the Coast Guard isn't that careless. The perps either arrived by dinghy or some other kind of boat they tied to the ladder. They massacre everyone on board except for Janice and Kresley. Then get back in their boat and leave?"

"I know," Gabe agreed, reading his mind. "There's no such animal as a nautical spree killer. There had to be something on the *Carolina Moon* that was worth killing for."

"Drugs, guns, human trafficking," Matt clicked off. "Hell, it could be gold or pretty much anything you could fit in the hold."

"It would be nice if Kresley could remember what happened."

Matt let out a humorless laugh. "Tell me about it."

After he hung up the phone, he had the unpleasant task of telling Kresley her roommates were dead. She nodded and sat on the sofa, staring straight ahead. Tears slipped unchecked down her cheeks.

KRESLEY WASN'T fully awake when the images hit her. A bloody, mangled, terrifying flash of memories played like a PowerPoint presentation in her brain. A man and a woman, dressed head to toe in black. A shiny serrated knife held in a black gloved hand. Screaming, lots of screaming.

She sat up with a start. Confused and disoriented. Where was she? Perspiration trickled between her breasts as she reached for the lamp on the bedside table. Just as she found the switch, her cell phone rang.

"Hello?"

"Bring it to Waterfront Park. Alone. Thirty minutes or you're dead."

Chapter Six

"Matt!" she called as she leapt off the bed and went racing into the living room, flipping on lights as she went.

She'd already wasted one of the minutes she'd been given by the threatening male voice.

She was alone in the apartment. On the coffee table, Matt had leaned a notepad up to display the phone number. Taking out her cell, her fingers trembled as she dialed the number.

"DeMarco."

Just the sound of his voice calmed her. She didn't need a memory to know that going to Waterfront Park, alone, in the dark was a dumb idea. She could hear traffic, then the opening and closing of a door in the background as she told him about the call. "Where are you?"

"Walking through the Rose Tattoo. I'll be there in a few seconds."

Kresley flipped her phone closed and then went to the window and peeked between the wooden slats on the plantation shutters. Her heart was pounding and she was battling the very strong urge to cry. Between no memory, being shot at, the vivid, bloody dream and now a threatening phone call, she was on the verge of a complete meltdown.

She watched Matt jog across the well-lit parking area and timed opening the door perfectly.

Matt had his phone to his ear. "…follow us." He closed his phone as his blue eyes scanned her face. He reached over and rested his palm against her cheek. "I'm sorry I wasn't here for you."

"That doesn't matter. He said—"

Matt moved his finger to her lips. "Shush and take a breath. I know what he said." Slowly his finger slipped away from her mouth.

"How?"

"I cloned your phone. I heard his voice and his instructions."

"How do you— Forget it. I swear, I don't know what it is he's talking about."

"If I had to guess, I'd say it was whatever was taped to your torso."

Kresley's heart rate quickened. "That's at the bottom of the Atlantic, right?"

"Probably."

Matt hurried toward the second bedroom. The bed was pushed up against the far side of the room and several black cases were stacked neatly against the wall. A good third of the bed was covered with various knives and holsters and gun clips.

As soon as he opened the top case, Kresley sucked

in a breath. Inside a custom foam cut-out there was an intimidating looking gun. It looked like the guns she saw in movies only this one had a scope thing on the top. Just hearing the magazine click into place was enough to make her knees shake.

"You have an arsenal," she said, swallowing as he tucked the gun in the waistband of his jeans.

Then he strapped a holster to his ankle and put a smaller weapon inside the leather band. "Gabe and I will have you covered."

"Hang on. I'm going to Waterfront Park?"

"I agree this isn't optimal, but right now, it's the best we've got. We have to flush this guy out."

"I don't want to meet him."

"If he thinks you have what he wants, he won't kill you."

"Really? And you know this how?"

"The guy that shot at us from the SUV aimed high. He could have killed us both, but he didn't. He wanted to get your attention."

"Well, it worked."

Matt kissed her forehead. "I swear, Kresley, I've got your back."

"That's great. But who will have my sides and my front? I've already been shot and I didn't care for it much."

"Fine," Matt said as he leaned in the doorway and looked at his watch. "The guy expects to see you in eleven minutes or he'll probably make good on his threat."

A shiver danced along her spine. “So I’ll check into a hotel and hide.”

“Is that how you’re going to spend the rest of your life? Hiding?”

That didn’t sound like much of a life. Still she wasn’t in any hurry to get killed, either. Did the guy know her physical location? Or had he just dialed her cell number?

Relenting, she mumbled, “Let’s go,” and headed for the door.

“Hey,” he said, stopping her as she walked past him. “You can do this Kresley. I saw the yacht. If you fought your way out of that situation, you can do anything.”

During the short drive Kresley gave herself a mental pep talk. Matt pulled his Jeep down a small alley where a dark green Mercedes sat idling.

A tall, handsome man with long, dark hair pulled back with a narrow length of leather stepped out of the car and into the headlights. He had hazel eyes with catlike golden flecks, and a diamond stud sparkled from his left earlobe. For a large man, he moved with incredible grace.

“Gabe Langston,” he said, extending his hand. He wore jeans, a polo shirt, loafers and a perfect poker face.

Kresley absently took his hand, focused only on the idea that she might very well get killed.

“Ready?” he asked Matt.

Matt nodded. “How open is it?”

“Very. Which works to our advantage. I’ve got

guys covering two blocks in either direction for a mile. You can have this roof, I'll take the one across the street."

"How about you?" Gabe asked her.

She clutched her purse to her. "I'm just dandy. Can't think of a more relaxing way to spend an evening."

Matt gave her leg a squeeze. "You don't have to do this if you don't want to. We can—"

"I don't want to live terrified all the time. If this is what it will take to get rid of whoever wants me dead, then okay."

As unpleasant as it was, she walked the final block alone. The street was deserted save for a few cars. She saw a couple out of the corner of one eye. They were plastered up against a building making out. There was an elderly man seated on one of the benches, all his worldly possessions stacked in a grocery cart to his left.

Waterfront Park was straight ahead. She could almost make out the big bronze pineapple. Kresley tried to recall every horrific snippet of memory. In her mind's eye, a figure clad all in black appeared in silhouette, a man. It didn't matter how hard she pressed her brain, she couldn't bring any more detail to the image. The knife he carried was a completely different matter.

It was a sight she'd never forget. The handle was leather, the blade maybe seven or eight inches long. It wasn't the glint of the metal she remembered, but letters near the hilt. Four, the first two were US. Not much help.

"*Us* what?" she wondered aloud.

Her insides were all twisted with anticipation and a healthy dose of fear. Please let Matt and Gabe find her mysterious caller. If for no other reason than to tell Matt what had happened to Janice. But she wouldn't mind him sharing how she'd ended up in the water wearing a gazillion-dollar dress and a bullet hole.

Kresley reached the entrance of the park and stood right in front of the pineapple. Only a blind man would miss her standing there. While she didn't have a watch, she did have her purse open and could read the time on her cell phone. Every minute took a lifetime. Her heart beat faster as she watched the time click to the precise moment she was supposed to meet the creepy man.

She was breathing deeply, trying to hold her panic in abeyance. Every branch that moved, every palm frond that swayed made her jump. *Maybe this wasn't such a good idea,* she thought.

Kresley stood there, watching time pass, and pass some more. Creepy guy was over an hour late. Or he'd seen Gabe or Matt or one of the other people and changed plans. She shifted her weight to the other foot when a wave of *something* washed over her, putting her just off-balance enough that she placed her right hand on the sculpture to steady herself. The stitches pinched from the motion, but her head was literally swimming in a dense fog. Knees weak, she leaned against the pineapple.

She saw red, not blood-red, more like fire-engine

red, with flashing red lights. Then she smelled it. Sea water. Then tasted it. Briny, salty ocean mixed with river water. But she wasn't in the water. At least she didn't think so. She didn't have the feeling of weightlessness that came from being in the water.

Squeezing her lids tightly, she heard laughter and the clinking of glasses. Champagne bubbles tickled her nose. She was standing next to a woman, someone she knew. Only she couldn't shake it free from her brain. The short-haired, tall, lanky brunette's name was right there on the tip of her tongue but it stubbornly refused to cooperate.

She heard her name, softly at first, then louder and louder. Then the blonde was screaming, "Kresley! Kres…" she turned in time to see the man in black slit the blonde's throat, nearly decapitating her.

Her stomach lurched but Kresley forced herself to continue reliving the scene. She dropped the champagne flute and ran toward the front of the boat. Her companions weren't as fast. The man with the knife murdered them one by one.

She stepped up onto the first rung of the railing, looking down into the black abyss of the ocean below. Glancing over her shoulder, she knew she didn't have time to climb two more rungs, then up and over the polished teak railing.

Using all her might, she hoisted up yards of material and did half a rotation, kicking her would-be killer in the jaw.

He fell to the ground, the knife skittering across the deck. Kresley heard a moan from the back of the boat just as she was about to jump into the water. She couldn't leave whoever it was to die alone.

The figure in black lay face down on the deck, as still as a stone. Kresley made the split-second decision to make a move for the knife. She knew the roundhouse kick had only immobilized the man. As soon as her hand grasped the handle, his palm closed over her, his fingers prying loose her grip.

Kresley's brain knew he was slicing her hand as he reclaimed the knife, however, adrenaline kept her from feeling the pain. His knee came up and caught her in the midsection, sending her careening into the railing. Something around her chest pulled, but she ignored the odd sensation as she prepared for his next move.

Though he had at least a hundred pounds on her, she had determination on her side. And serious motivation—she didn't want to die.

As she had done so often at the dojo, Kresley timed the snap kick accurately. It was fast and it struck him right in the sternum. He stumbled back, falling onto his butt.

Kresley raced over to the opposite side of the boat, ducking under ropes and riggings. The kick wouldn't incapacitate her attacker for long. Sidestepping the opening to the hold below, she found herself at the stern of the yacht… The red was back, strobing and blinding as she looked out at the otherwise black horizon.

Hearing a noise behind her, she spun just in time to see her attacker plunging the knife toward her.

Using her left hand, she made a blocking motion to deflect the blade. Her hand slipped, allowing the blade to slice her skin again.

The flashing red lights grew closer as she continued to fight for her life. Rotating her body, she landed another kick that sent the man and the knife flying. The knife flipped end over end, landing in the water with a splash. All she had to do was hold him at bay until the harbor police arrived.

Kresley got to her feet and again started toward the back of the boat where she knew there was a ladder. The deck was slippery with blood and littered bodies. A woman weakly called her name. Glancing back, she saw her attacker still rolling around clutching his throat so she crouched down next to a blonde who was pressing her hands to her stomach. Blood leeched through her fingers, staining the dress and eventually pooling on the deck.

"I'm sorry," she said. "I should have warned you."

"It's okay, Emma," Kresley said, gently lifting strands of hair from her face. "Help's almost here. Just hang on."

"Be—"

"Be what?" Kresley asked, leaning closer to Emma.

"Be-behind you."

Kresley stood and as she did, she did a hard back kick, hoping she'd hit something.

She did.

Wincing, Matt grabbed his shin and gritted his teeth as pain seared through his system. "What. The. Hell. Was. That. For?"

Kresley turned, her blue eyes wide, her cheeks stained with tears. "I—I'm so sorry," she said, still a tad disoriented.

He hobbled for a second or two, continually rubbing his shin.

"Geez, what'd you hit me with, steel-toed boots?"

"Why are you here?" she whispered, her eyes darting around in the darkness. "If he sees you he won't show."

"He's not going to show. Something spooked him. Is that what happened to you?" Matt asked. "I signaled you twice from the rooftop and you didn't respond. You scared the crap out of me." He stopped ranting and looked at her. "Want to tell me why you've been crying?"

Unashamedly, she swiped her cheeks with the back of her right hand. "Didn't know I was."

"Something upset you enough to make you cry and kick the shi-*heck* out of me."

"I remembered a lot about the other night. I remember being on the yacht."

Matt's pulse quickened. "Did you see Janice there?"

"I got a flash of Janice, I think. I don't remember her being there when the horrible stuff started. I remember seeing a man dressed in all black, could have been a wet suit," she said as if the thought had just occurred to her.

"Yes?" Matt prompted when she fell silent.

"He had a big knife and went person to person, slicing and stabbing."

"Where were you?"

"I ran to the front of the boat. I was going to jump, but he caught up to me."

"Shoulda kicked him the way you kicked me."

"I did," Kresley said, sounding amazed. "I fought him and fought him. I used everything I learned at every dojo and gym in the greater Charleston area. Even after he cut my hand."

"So that thing you just did," Matt said, rolling his fingers. "You were reliving what happened on the boat?"

"I guess. I really am sorry, can I take a look?"

"It's nothing," Matt insisted.

"What can I do to help?"

"Let's go home," he said.

He cradled her face in his palm while his thumb gently erased the tracks of her tears. What had started out as a purely innocent gesture changed when he felt the sensation of her warm breath tickle the back of his hand. His gaze dropped to her mouth. "What you did tonight took a lot of guts," he said softly. She had full soft lips that practically insisted he kiss her.

Instead, he drew the pad of his thumb over her bottom lip. A soft, feathery pass. He was fascinated when her tongue flicked out to remoisten her lip. His second pass wasn't quite as gentle and there was nothing feathery about the way he used his thumb to simulate a passionate kiss. He let his fingers do what his lips could not.

Her breathing became uneven and shallow. That only served to fan the flames of his growing desire.

His timing couldn't be worse, but Matt's need-addled brain didn't seem to be listening to reason. He just knew that his heart quickened when she made that little noise when he touched her upper lip. And his body predictably stiffened when she surprised him by lifting her hand to his face.

Her small, delicate fingers traced the outline of his jaw, stopping only to toy with the cleft in his chin. He could feel the scrape from the day's growth of beard against her fingernails.

"We're getting into dangerous territory," he warned.

"Not interested?" she asked softly.

He cocked his head to one side. "Does it look like I'm not interested?"

"No. Then why?"

Matt dropped his hand to grab her wrist. "You've been shot, stabbed, shot at again and threatened by some maniac over the phone. I think that's enough excitement for a while." He started back to where he'd parked the Jeep, bringing her with him. "Ouch. Oh yeah, and there's the minor detail that you almost broke my leg."

"Really?" she cried.

"No," he said, gripping her so he could place a kiss on the top of her head.

Chapter Seven

Kresley slept fitfully and woke early. Not as early as Matt, who was seated at the small table adjacent to the kitchen, sipping a mug of coffee when she walked in.

After a short discussion, they decided that she'd be safer staying at his place. Just because the creepy guy hadn't shown up last night didn't mean he wouldn't turn up at her apartment.

Matt's hair was mussed and a shadow of dark beard covered his chin. Most disconcerting, he was shirtless. Gloriously naked from the waist up. He was all tanned and taut muscle. Short, dark, curly hair covered his chest, tapering down into a thin line before disappearing into the waistband of his jeans. It pretty much acted like a big arrow saying, 'This way! This way!'

She managed to avoid the invitation. Barely.

His gaze met hers. "What can I get for you? Coffee, juice?"

You. "Coffee sounds great."

When he stood up and walked the short distance to the antiquated percolator, Kresley was relieved to see he wasn't limping. "How's your leg?"

"Ice and ibuprofen cures almost anything."

Taking the seat opposite him, she felt a little awkward. Okay, a *lot* awkward. He was half-dressed and she was wearing a sports bra, thin T-shirt and ladies' boxers. It was a very domestic scene, except that she knew virtually nothing about him and not much more about herself.

Matt placed a steaming mug in front of her, then sat back down. Kresley took one sip and had to fight to keep from gagging. "This will put hair on your chest," she said.

"Sorry. I like it on the strong side. I can make another pot."

"No, just some cream or milk please?"

He got the cream and Kresley poured a quick stream into her mug. The coffee didn't change color; it remained as black as tar. Reluctantly, she drank more of the sludge, then topped the cup off with as much cream as it would hold. It wasn't great but it was caffeine, and that was enough.

"Anything interesting?" she asked, trying to peer around the newspaper.

"I was just looking to see if there was anything about the yacht or the shooting."

"And?"

He folded the newspaper and placed it on the small table. "A brief article on the yacht, two lines in the Crime Beat about the shooting on Queen Street."

"I remembered another detail. Or I dreamed it," she admitted. "It's hard to tell where my dreams end and my actual memories begin." She told him about Emma. About the apology and about seeing the harbor police coming toward the boat.

"What came to you last night?"

"It's a little disjointed," she admitted as she forced down another sip of too-strong coffee. "One minute I was in my classroom, having the kids read aloud when there was a knock at the door. I opened it and suddenly I was back on the yacht."

"That is one weird dream."

"I was standing on top of the railing, watching the red harbor police strobe lights reflect off the ocean. I jumped."

"Wait a sec. Last night you said you stayed on the boat and fought the guy. Now you remember that you jumped off the boat even though you could see the flashing lights from a rescue vessel?" Matt repeated. "Why would you do that?"

She shook her head and inched the coffee mug closer to the center of the table. "I clearly remember hitting the wave and how much it stung my hand. I clearly remember telling myself over and over to swim. Swim faster and faster. Then I felt a sharp pain under my right arm."

"That sounds like you were shot after you jumped off the boat."

Kresley shrugged. "Could be. That isn't the weirdest part though."

"It's right up there."

"I could see the lights from the harbor patrol and hear the engine and smell the diesel fuel. I think the harbor-patrol boat was tied to the yacht when I dove in."

Matt's brow furrowed. "You've got to have that part confused. The harbor patrol didn't find the boat, the Coast Guard did. The yacht was adrift for more than twenty-four hours. I found you before the Coast Guard found the boat."

Kresley pressed the heels of her hands against her eyes. Her wounded left hand immediately responded by sending a shooting pain up her arm. "I know. But I swear another boat was tied alongside the yacht."

"That would explain the red paint transfer."

"What?"

"When they processed the yacht after it was towed in, they found a scrape of paint on the hull."

"Why didn't you tell me?"

"Because when you were unconscious Kendall told me it was better if you remembered things at your own pace. Look on the bright side, you're getting your memory back."

"That is a plus," Kresley agreed.

"Why don't you take the shower first?" Matt suggested.

"Are we going someplace?"

"I thought we'd take a run back to your place so you could pack a suitcase. Or you can keep borrowing clothes from Shelby. Hey," he said with a smile, "maybe Rose will share those leopard stretch pants."

He must have seen the flare of fear in her eyes because he asked, “Would you rather stay here?”

“I’d rather understand why the guy called me, threatened me and then didn’t show up. Does that happen often?”

Matt shrugged. “Yeah. They see something that spooks them. I’m sure he’ll make contact again. If he’s willing to kill for it, you must have had something very important to him.”

“You think it was a tape recorder?”

Matt sat back, lacing his fingers behind his head. “Yes. It fits the amount of duct tape. I’m just trying to figure out why you’d be wearing the wire when Janice was on the boat.”

“Maybe they were suspicious of Janice so she asked one of us to wear it. Emma did apologize to me, maybe she was supposed to wear it but changed her mind? It would explain why she apologized.”

“Any memory about the male guests?” Matt asked. “There were eight guests, the captain and a porter. Prints identified you, Janice and your two roommates. They matched the prints of the two men found on board as well as the captain and the porter. That leaves two sets of prints unaccounted for. Size and width suggests the unknowns were male.”

“Sorry,” she said on a breath. “It’s frustrating not being able to remember.”

Kresley placed her mug in the sink, then went and took a shower. She had no option but to wear the capris and top she’d worn the day before. It didn’t matter, she could change once they got to her apartment. What did matter, a little at least, was her total lack of makeup. She had dark circles under her eyes and her lips were dry and sunburned.

After dressing she put her phone in the purse. Weird that having a purse would make her feel so...*normal.*

THIS WAS definitely not normal, Matt thought as he lathered shampoo in his hair. Kresley was his best and only lead to finding Janice. Keeping her close until her memory returned was an easy, straightforward task. Except that he wanted her. Bad.

He leaned into the spray, his palms flat against the cool tiles. With his eyes closed, his thoughts instantly went to what he wanted most. He imagined her mouth would be warm and pliant. He'd kiss her until she went weak in the knees. He'd gotten a glimpse of what passion did to her eyes. They went from bright to a smoky, seductive blue. The image of running his hands all over her body made him groan. He'd gotten a teasing glimpse of her legs when he'd fished her out of the surf. She had a small mole on her inner thigh that begged to be kissed. The low-cut gown revealed generous breasts that seemed made for his hands.

Matt sighed and pushed away from the wall. He shaved, hoping the task would redirect his thoughts. The plan worked marginally, and that would have to do.

"Do you have to work today?" Kresley called through the door.

"Not today." Matt towel-dried his hair and himself and got dressed listening to the sound of her pacing. She was like a caged animal and he genuinely felt for her. If the tables were turned, he'd be going nuts.

She was so lost in her thoughts that she didn't make the pivot in time as he opened the bathroom door. Suddenly she was pressed against him. The heat from her body mirrored the heat burning in the pit of his stomach.

Matt bracketed her shoulders, dipped his head and looked into her eyes. This was one of those moments when life just blindsides you. He could be heroic and strong and walk away. Or, he could be a normal human being with all the normal responses.

HIS LIPS BRUSHED against the sensitive skin just below her earlobe. The feel of his feather-light kisses drew her stomach into a knot of anticipation. Closing her eyes, Kresley concentrated on the glorious sensations. His grip tightened as his tongue traced a path up to her ear. Her breath caught when he teasingly nibbled the edge of her lobe.

His hands traveled upward and rested against her rib cage. She swallowed the moan rumbling in her throat. She was aware of everything—his fingers, the feel of his solid body molded against hers, the magical kisses.

"You smell wonderful," he said against her heated skin.

"Matt," she whispered his name. "I don't think this is such a good idea."

His mouth stilled and he gripped her waist, turning her in his arms. His eyes were thickly lashed and hooded. A lock of his damp, jet-black hair had fallen forward and rested just above his brows. His chiseled mouth was curved in an effortlessly sexy half smile. "You're right. I can't seem to help myself."

He applied pressure to the middle of her back, urging her closer to him.

"We shouldn't do this," she managed above her rapid heartbeat.

"I know," he agreed, punctuating his remark with a kiss on her forehead. "Problem is, I look at you and I can't think of anything *but* this."

His palms slid up her back until he cradled her face in his hands. Using his thumbs, Matt tilted her head back and hesitated only fractionally before his mouth found hers. Instinctively, Kresley's hands went to his waist.

The scent of soap and cologne filled her nostrils as the exquisite pressure of his mouth increased. His fingers began to massage their way toward her spine until the tips began a slow, sensual counting of each vertebra. Her mind was no longer capable of rational thought. All her attention was honed on the intense sensations filling her with fierce desire.

She reveled in the feel of his strong body against hers. As he deepened the kiss into something more demanding, she succumbed to the potent dose of longing.

She began to explore the solid contours of his

body beneath his soft cotton shirt. It was like feeling the smooth, sculpted surface of granite. Everywhere she touched she felt the distinct outline of corded muscle.

When he lifted his head, she had to fight to keep from giving in to her strong urge to pull him back to her. His eyes met and held hers as he quietly looked down, searching her face. His breaths were coming in short, raspy gulps and she watched the tiny vein at his temple race in time with her own rapid heartbeat.

"I've never done this," he said.

Kresley's eyes flew open wider and her expression must have registered obvious shock.

Matt's laugh was deep and reached his eyes.

"I mean I've done *this,*" he corrected. "I've just never had to be so completely restrained before."

"How's it working out for you?"

"Not that well," he said as he claimed her mouth again. His kiss lasted for several heavenly moments. "As much as I love the way your mouth feels, I agree, this is a bad idea." He hooked his thumb under her chin and forced her to meet his eyes.

She tried to ignore the sudden tightness in the pit of her stomach. But she couldn't ignore the sudden ringing of the cell phone on the coffee table.

"DeMarco," he answered, one hand still resting on her neck, his forefinger making erotic little circles.

"We'll be right there," he said a moment later.

"What?"

"Gabe found something interesting in your bank account."

She winced. "I paid the nasty landlady the rent. Am I overdrawn?"

"Far from it. The night of the cruise someone wired five grand into your account."

Chapter Eight

Kresley followed Matt as he turned north after exiting the front door of the Rose Tattoo. The street was uneven; some of the original brick still showed through the layers of macadam. The air was fresh and warm and she could smell the remnants of night jasmine on the slight breeze. The sun warmed her shoulders and the exposed back of her neck because she'd twisted her hair up.

There were no storm drains and every house seemed to have a metal medallion placed on the second floor. "What are those?"

Matt looked to where she pointed. "Earthquake bolts."

"In Charleston?"

"After the 1886 earthquake, people decided that bolting their houses to the frames was a good idea."

"Was it?"

"They're still standing more than a hundred years later." Matt paused, and waved his arm toward a wrought-iron arbor covered with variegated ivy.

There was a small metal sign, slightly obscured by the plant that read, Langston Investigations.

Kresley guessed if one wanted discreet, this was a place that fit the bill perfectly. Matt walked in without knocking. There was an empty desk—probably for a receptionist, and a closed door sporting a Private sign. Kresley smelled coffee and cinnamon and her mouth began to water.

Without concern for the sign, Matt walked right into Gabe's office. It didn't appear to bother the other man. The office was large, with a massive mahogany desk and matching file cabinets. Sprinkled everywhere was evidence of his family. Too many photographs of a cute little girl with fiery red hair to count. Almost as many of the stunning redhead, including one photo of Gabe and the redhead on their wedding day.

He stood when they entered, reaching around Matt and taking Kresley's hand. "Matt tells me you're getting your memory back."

She shrugged. "In fits and starts."

Gabe took his seat, rolling it forward as he opened an ultra-thin laptop. Spinning it, he showed her the screen with her banking information.

After removing her sunglasses, she stared at it, suddenly getting a flash of an image. She was standing at the teller's window, her check card and driver's license in her hand. Closing her eyes, she focused on the bank's lobby, finally seeing a calendar on the shelf next to the teller. The memory coincided with the date someone put five thousand dollars into her account.

These little trips down fragmented memory lane left her feeling exhausted. She sat down on a brown, butter-soft leather chair and pressed her fingers against her temple. Matt took the seat next to her, his large hand casually resting on her thigh. She was fighting battles on two fronts. She was trying so hard to remember and just as hard to forget the way his kiss had left her wanting so much more.

"Ringing any bells?" Gabe asked as he retied the length of brown leather holding his ponytail.

"I was definitely at the bank the day of the cruise," Kresley said. "I think I was checking the balance in my account."

"So you were expecting the transfer from an offshore account?" Gabe asked in a reasonable tone.

Kresley had a suspicion that while Gabe Langston seemed harmless enough, he wasn't the kind of man you wanted to cross. There was something about his controlled, measured tone that made her think he would and could attack when necessary. That and his tight polo shirt that revealed well-developed biceps and cement-solid abs. It would take a lot for someone to get the better of this guy in a fight.

"I must have been. I just can't think of a reason why I'd be getting five thousand dollars from anyone. I don't have any family and I can't imagine a friend raining five thousand dollars down on my head."

Gabe turned the laptop back around and his square-tipped fingers flew across the keyboard. "I did a little hacking and it turns out your friends were getting offshore deposits, too."

"My friends?"

"Roommates," Gabe clarified. "Abigail Howell and Emma Rooper have similar deposit patterns that go back nearly a year. Five-grand deposits, followed by a second five-grand deposit a day later. They were into something illegal, I traced the offshore account. Know anyone named Paula Nelson?"

"She was my maid of honor and my fiancé's bed buddy until a month ago." Kresley answered. "Why?"

"Until a month ago, she was getting the same two payments."

"Why two?" Kresley murmured.

Matt squeezed her leg gently, and then said, "By breaking up the deposits, they avoided the banking laws that require reporting deposits of ten thousand or more to the IRS. People don't usually dodge the IRS unless they have something to hide."

Kresley swallowed nervously, afraid to ask the question, but had no choice. "Was I doing it, too?"

Gabe shook his head. "I went back a year. Looks like the deposit you made three days ago was your first and last."

"There was no second transfer?" Matt asked.

"No. Not for Kresley or her roommates. Whoever was playing sugar daddy knew they wouldn't be around to collect the five grand on the other end."

A shiver raced along her spine. "But there is someone left we can ask."

"Who?"

Kresley stood and began to pace. "Paula and David moved out of state, right?"

Matt nodded, turning to Gabe and giving him a brief outline.

"Gimme that last name again," Gabe asked as his fingers hovered above his keyboard.

"Avery," Kresley said, without feeling an iota of emotion.

"That's interesting," he said after a prolonged silence.

"What?" Kresley and Matt asked in unison.

"David Avery and Paula Nelson died in a house fire last night," Gabe said, then twisted the screen so they could see the headline.

"That's a coincidence," Kresley said. She wasn't sure how she felt. Numb maybe. These two people had betrayed her. Now they were dead. Very unsettling.

"Too much so if you ask me," Matt agreed. "Anything relevant in the details?"

"Yes," Gabe answered. "The fire department in Fayetteville, North Carolina, got the call four hours and fifteen minutes after Kresley got her call."

"I don't understand," Kresley said.

"I think we just found out why your night caller was a no-show. Your caller was busy committing arson. It's roughly two hundred and twenty miles one way. The time frame fits."

"How would the guy who threatened me know about Paula?"

"Best guess?" Gabe asked. "He's the one writing the checks. Or maybe he works for the guy writing the checks. Bottom line is neither Matt nor I have been able to tie you, Janice, Emma, Abby and Paula together except for your apartment and these deposits."

"Gabe and his guys copied all the license plates in the area of the park last night," Matt said, then turned his attention to Gabe. "Anything come of that?"

"I started with the SUVs, three black, one midnight blue. Of the four parked in the lot, the dark-blue one belongs to a tourist from Savannah and the other three are government issue. Two are registered to the park service and one to the harbor patrol. I tracked them down this morning and all of them have verifiable alibis for the time Kresley got the call and for the hour following."

"I think the harbor-patrol guy is worth a second look," Kresley said.

"The SUV was signed out to a woman, not a man. Mary Jestrzebeski. But I can check again. Why harbor patrol?"

Kresley recounted her dream, now certain that she'd seen the red strobe lights of a rescue boat tied to the stern. "Maybe the harbor patrol was part of whatever was happening on that yacht. It's worth a second look, right?"

Gabe's mouth curved into a frown. "Tom Whitford, he's the local Coast Guard Commander, he was with the female harbor-patrol officer at the time you got the call. I've known Tom since I moved to Charleston and I can't see him lying to protect Mary. She's only been with the HP for a year."

Gabe seemed so certain that Kresley kept her concerns to herself. Well, they weren't concerns so much as that nagging feeling that buried somewhere in Gabe's comments was something important.

"Can you find out who was working the harbor on the night everyone was…was…"

Gabe smiled at her. "Consider it done. I'll track down every boat in the vicinity."

"Thanks. There's a third link," Kresley said as she clutched her purse and stood. "The gowns. I think now would be a good time to visit Gianni's salon."

"I can do that," Matt said. "I'd rather you stayed locked in my apartment."

"I'm sure you would. But there's a chance that hearing his voice or seeing his face will trigger more memories."

"I could discreetly snap a photo of him with my phone and tape him speaking."

"Not the—" Kresley stopped in midsentence as a series of pictures ran through her head. "I had a tape," she suddenly remembered.

"What?"

"It was a small voice recorder."

"You had that on the boat?" Matt asked.

She looked apologetically from Gabe to Matt. "I remember having it in my hand."

"You had duct-tape residue on your body, so at some point it wasn't in your hand," Matt said.

"Well," Kresley spoke as she paced, barely aware of the fact that she was speaking aloud. "If—and this is a big if—I was wearing a tape recorder under my gown, maybe the great Gianni did some alterations to accommodate the recorder."

"Then let's go back to where we know it starts. Maybe if we learn how you got that gown, it will lead us to what you got caught up in."

Gabe reached into his pocket and tossed Matt a set of keys. "Take my car, it's parked in the back alley."

"Can't we walk?" Kresley asked.

Matt scoffed. "Yeah, 'cause that worked out really well the last time."

"If someone's watching you, they'll be on the lookout for the Jeep. I'll keep on those license plates. Maybe something useful will turn up."

"Thanks," Matt said, moving around the desk to give his friend one of those mannish fist bump things.

Kresley stood waiting, her own skin still tingling from Matt's touch. Odd that her entire past was a mishmash of images, but her awareness of Matt was perfectly honed.

She remembered the feel of his mouth on hers and wanted more. The feel of his hands on her body and wanted more. Even now, with so much up in the air, she could happily have gone back to his apartment to make love.

The mere thought of a lazy afternoon tangled in his sheets, studying every inch of his body made her weak in the knees. She should be focusing all her energies on remembering her murky past, yet there she was, longing to run her hands through his thick, dark hair. Or have him close enough so she could smell his woodsy cologne. It was as if all her senses were heightened when Matt was near.

"Let's go meet Gianni," Matt said, absently placing his hand at the small of her back. Kresley felt the breadth of his palm, the splay of his fingers and her pulse quickened.

Going out the back of the building, they headed toward the dark-green Mercedes parked in the alleyway. Matt pressed a button on the keychain and the car chirped while the lights flashed.

Kresley abruptly stopped.

"What?" he asked.

Not wanting to lose the snippet of memory, Kresley closed her eyes, remembering more about her roommates. Emma and Abby were no longer merely names. She got into the passenger's seat, and then murmured, "Why would I have issues with them? We lived together. We obviously socialized together or I wouldn't have been on that yacht. But I didn't like them."

"Did you have a fight or something?" Matt asked before started the engine. "Understandable, four women sharing a pretty small apartment."

Kresley tapped her fingernail against her chin. "It was about the apartment."

In her mind she heard angry, raised voices. She heard Emma—the same Emma who'd apologized to her as she lay dying on the deck—calling her a deadbeat. Kresley remembered feeling guilty and frustrated as Abby and Emma took turns berating her for being so far behind on her rent.

"They didn't like me, either," Kresley admitted. "Or more accurately, they didn't like that I was behind on my rent. Apparently when I was teaching, I was fine but once I quit to go to grad school, I was having a hard time keeping up with my obligations."

"That might explain why you got involved with whatever they had going on."

"Do you remember what they did for a living? God," she ran her hands over her hair. "Now I can't remember something you told me yesterday."

"You've had a lot on your plate," Matt said. "Abby was a waitress at The Grille in Summerville. And Emma worked for a pawn shop, Treasures Pawn Shop off Spring Street."

"And me?"

"In the last two years you've been substitute teaching and waitressing," Matt paused to glance at her, grinning from ear to ear. "And you did three months as a part-time grocery checker at Piggly Wiggly."

"No wonder they were irritated with me. Sounds like I couldn't keep a job."

"No, it sounds like the job history of a full-time grad student."

It took less time to drive to Gianni's salon than it did to find a parking spot. One reason could have been the big glazier's truck double-parked in front of the shop with the shot-out window. Kresley shivered, remembering how close she'd been to death.

After they'd circled the block six times, a spot

opened up about ten feet from the salon. Kresley still felt as if something important was just on the tip of her consciousness but no more memory flashes appeared.

They entered the salon and a faint chime echoed through the elegant room. Kresley smelled lavender competing with a strong men's cologne that reached her about a second before Gianni came out from behind the heavy curtain to the left of the stage.

He reminded her of Truman Capote: white suit, pastel shirt, pastel striped tie and white Italian tasseled loafers.

"How may I assist you?" he said in a thick, cultured southern accent.

Kresley smiled as she looked at him steadily. "Do you remember me?"

Gianni leaned back slightly and gave her a once-over. "One of the *girls*."

"*Girls?* What does that mean?" Kresley asked.

Gianni pretended to adjust the shine on his buffed nails. "You were the new girl," he said. "You came in with a brunette, about six feet tall with a ghastly, short butch haircut."

"Was her name Janice?" Kresley asked. "And you're sure we were together?"

Gianni seemed annoyed at having his recollection challenged. "Not only am I sure, but I have the receipt for the gown and the alteration."

"Alteration?"

Gianni rolled his eyes. "Your tall friend insisted the gown be a loose six when you are clearly a size four. She wouldn't listen even though I explained that that particular gown was made to hug a woman's body like a lover."

"The receipt?" Matt prompted.

"It's in my office. Wait here while I retrieve it."

Matt grabbed Kresley by the shoulders, turning her and meeting her eyes with a sense of urgency.

She was smiling. "Finally."

He glanced down at his watch. "How long does it take to find a receipt?"

"Gianni is an *artiste,* he probably can't balance his checkbook."

"Let's hope the woman's name is on the receipt. If it is, it would be the first tangible piece of evidence that Janice had uncovered whatever your friends were into."

Her smile evaporated. "Not just my friends. I got paid, too. Whatever they were doing, I was doing."

"I didn't mean for it to come out like that," Matt said. "And since we know you were the one wearing a wire, you had to be working for the good guys."

She stared up at him. "Let's hope. We should maybe go check on Gianni?" she suggested.

"Or we could pass the time some other way." He leaned over to kiss her, but she sidestepped him.

"Not an option," she said, turning her back on him.

"Give me five minutes and I bet I could change your mind."

"You could probably change it in three, which is why I want you to stay at least two feet behind me."

"Anyone ever tell you you're no fun?"

"I have no idea," she said with a pathetic little laugh. Walking to the back of the store, she pushed the curtain aside, she called, "Mr. Gianni?"

No response.

Neat rows of rolling racks filled the space behind the staging area. Two were nothing but wedding gowns and the other four were couture. Like any self-respecting woman, Kresley couldn't help but ogle the designs.

"Hey! Gianni!" Matt called.

In the far back of the building, Kresley spotted a door marked Exit and another one marked Office. The exit door was ajar.

Fear surged through her. Matt moved in front of her, gun drawn, using his body to shield hers.

"Crap," he said as he opened the office door.

Gianni was sitting at his desk with a single bullet hole to the right of his eyebrow.

Chapter Nine

"I don't suppose there's any chance he isn't dead, is there?" Kresley asked.

Matt glanced at her and saw all the color had drained from her face. "No, he's gone," he said as he placed two fingers against the man's throat. "Be careful not to touch anything. My guess is a .22 based on the entry wound."

"Wasn't I shot with a .22?"

"Yep."

"So, three days ago someone shot at me and today someone shot at Gianni with the same gun? How come he didn't come through the showroom and shoot me? And how come we didn't hear the shot?"

"You must not have been the target. *This time.* As for why we didn't hear a shot, the shooter used a silencer."

Using a pencil, Matt sorted though the items on Gianni's desk, then turned to face her. "Wanna give me a hand searching the place?"

Kresley walked over to the file cabinet and lifted the hem of her shirt to pull the drawer out.

Matt was more than distracted at the sight of her bare midriff. Her hipbones protruded slightly, creating sexy curves that bracketed her flat stomach. Just a hint of her lacy bra was visible, but it was enough to ignite heat in his veins.

It wasn't as if he'd never seen a woman's body before. He'd just never wanted a woman as much as he wanted Kresley. Anything and everything about her intrigued him: the slightly husky sound of her voice, the way her every emotion was evident in her eyes, the subtle smell of her perfume, the graceful slope of her throat and the silky feel of her blond hair. Normally these were all things he would blot out when he was working a case. But there was something about this woman that commanded and controlled his attention.

"I found a J. Cross." Kresley said. "She ordered a gown a week before the yacht left port. Size six. Had one fitting and picked it up the morning the *Carolina Moon* sailed."

Matt came over and took the file. "That's Janice's signature," he said. Raking his hands through his hair, he added, "This has to be a credit card number," he added.

"Are we—"

"Shush," Matt said, placing his forefinger against her lips. "Hear that?"

"Sirens."

"Time to leave," he said, grabbing Janice's file

and closing the drawers with his elbow. "Out the back."

Matt took her on a confusing race down alleys and up and over small fenced yards as they made their way back to the Rose Tattoo. He didn't slow down until they'd got to his apartment. Kresley was a little out of breath, but nothing major.

She bent forward, resting her right hand on her knee as she breathed deeply and convinced her heart to return to normal rhythm. "Okay, so what now?"

"We see if Gabe can trace the credit card and do a reverse directory check on the phone number."

Unlocking the door, they entered his apartment and Matt went right the kitchen and grabbed two bottles of water out of the fridge.

He held one out for Kresley. She rolled the bottle against her forehead, then lifted her hair off her neck and rested the bottle there for a few seconds.

"Sorry, I shouldn't have pushed you so hard."

She shook her head as she twisted the cap off the bottle. "It wasn't a big deal."

Her cell phone rang and she reached into her purse, retrieved it and pressed the speaker button. "Hello?"

"I'm giving you one more chance, Miss Hayes. Meet me at the west end of the market at 6:00 p.m. tonight. We'll make the transfer then."

After the distinctive click, Kresley turned the phone and showed Matt the caller ID. Blocked.

"Great." A few seconds later, Matt's phone rang. It was Gabe. "It's a throwaway."

"I was afraid of that," Matt admitted, with a frustrated sigh.

"Have a little faith. Just because it's a disposable doesn't mean I can't triangulate off the cell towers and give you a general idea of where the call originated. I can also hit up my contact with the cell company and find out where the phone was purchased."

"I've got a credit card number on a receipt I'd like you to trace ASAP," Matt said. He read the numbers to Gabe then hung up.

"I'm glad you cloned the phone. That guy's voice makes my skin crawl."

"Sorry. Any new memory flashes after seeing Gianni?" he asked.

Kresley looked up into the full force of his eyes. He was so tall, his shoulders so broad that she could feel her pulse beginning to quicken. "I'm afraid my mind is still focused on the sight of him dead in the chair."

One dark brow arched and his mouth pulled into a straight line. "Try to think of something more pleasant."

"Like you being a federal agent?" she asked softly.

He reached for her with one hand, allowing it to rest on her shoulder, near her collarbone. She felt every inch of his squared fingers against her bare flesh. His touch wasn't nearly as powerful as the simmering passion in his sky-colored eyes.

The air between them felt palpable. It was as if a

current had engaged, filling the inches that separated them with a strong and powerful electricity. For several protracted seconds they both said nothing. She was too afraid of breaking the spell. She didn't know what might happen, but she didn't want to do anything that might disturb the bond joining them at that moment.

His eyes traveled lower, until she could almost feel him staring hard at her slightly parted lips. She knew instinctively that his thoughts were taking the same path as her own. His hand moved slowly toward her face, until he cupped her cheek, his thumb resting just inches from where his eyes remained riveted.

His thumb burned a path toward her lower lip. The intensity in his eyes deepened as his thumb brushed tentatively across her mouth. Forgetting the threatening caller for the moment; Kresley thought she might die from the anticipation knotting her stomach.

Raising her right hand, she flattened it against his chest. She could feel his heart beating against the solid muscle. A faint moan rumbled in his throat.

His head dipped fractionally closer and she waited eagerly, fully expecting and wanting his kiss. His thumb continued to work its magic. The friction had produced a heat that was carried to every cell in her body. Kresley swallowed.

"That first day, on the beach," he began in a husky, raspy voice.

"Yes?"

"When I said I wasn't interested."

"Yes?"

"I lied."

Gathering a handful of his T-shirt, Kresley urged him to her. His resistance was a surprise.

His eyes met and held hers. "It would be pretty low of me to take advantage of you now."

"I wouldn't consider it taking advantage," she told him.

Careful to avoid her injury, Matt drew her against him, cradling her head in his hand. His rapid heartbeat echoed her own.

"Well, I would," he said.

The first stirrings of embarrassment crept into her consciousness. She felt her face grow warm with the realization that she was prepared to beg the man if necessary.

"Let's swing by your apartment. I'm going to backtrack and get the Mercedes. Lock the door behind me and don't open it for anyone. Got it?"

"Not a problem, I'm in no hurry to die."

Matt was gone maybe thirty seconds when three sharp knocks at the door startled her. Kresley looked through the peephole. Rose was on the opposite side. She didn't know what to do.

"I know you're in there," Rose called.

Kresley turned the deadbolt and opened the door. "Hi," she greeted, trying to get a read on the woman.

Rose balanced a tray in one hand, carried it in, and set it on the table. Lifting the cloth napkin off the top, she said, "Chicken soup. Cures everything."

Surprised by the unexpected hospitality, Kresley stammered a thank-you.

Rose sat down on the sofa. Apparently she was staying a while. Kresley closed and locked the door, then joined the other woman. As usual, Rose had on an outlandish pair of animal-print leggings, mules with marabou accents and a skintight tube top.

Rose was eying her, sizing her up, but why?

"So, what do you think of Matt?"

"He's been very kind to me and—"

"Yeah, yeah. I know he's nice, I'm asking how you feel about him as a man."

Kresley mumbled, "I haven't thought much about that."

Rose pursed her cherry-red lips. "I don't care what kind of amnesia you've got, you'll never convince me that you forgot how to notice a man. It's not natural."

"He's very nice."

Rose groaned or grunted, or some weird combination of the two. "The guy who washes my car is very *nice,*" Rose said. "I'm just wondering if you've picked up on the way he looks at you?"

"How does he look at me?" Kresley asked, heart rate increasing.

"Like a man hungry for a woman."

Kresley's cheeks burned.

"Oh good God," Rose said impatiently. "Don't blush like a schoolgirl."

"I've known him for less than a week. What do you expect me to say? I'd like to marry him?"

"What's wrong with that?"

"Well, for starters, maybe I'm already in a relationship. Or, gee, maybe I think it's important to know someone before you contemplate commitment."

Rose shook her head and sighed deeply. "Ever heard of love at first sight?"

"Ever heard of a fifty-percent divorce rate?"

Rose cocked one penciled-in eyebrow. "If you're interested in the man, go for it."

"Why are we having this—forgive me—ridiculous conversation?"

"Because you and Matt are perfect for each other and I don't believe in standing on ceremony."

"Or…*dating*, apparently," Kresley said dryly.

Rose stood. "Eat the soup. We'll talk again soon."

For some time after Rose left the apartment, Kresley just stared at the door. Hands down, one of the strangest conversations of her life. She was about to eat when someone else knocked on the door.

This time when she looked through the peephole, Shelby was standing there, holding a small basket.

She opened the door. "Yes?"

Shelby offered a disarming smile that eased some of Kresley's discomfort. "I brought biscuits to go with your soup. Freshly baked."

They smelled wonderful and one peek told her they were flaky and buttery and probably a thousand calories a piece. "C'mon in."

Shelby did, sitting on the edge of the sofa, ankles crossed, hands folded in her lap. Like Matt, she had dark hair and an olive complexion that accentuated her brilliant blue eyes. On Matt, it was sexy. On Shelby, it was exotic.

"Are you the two in the one-two punch?" Kresley asked.

Shelby's smile broadened. "Rose means well. But she can be a bit...*opinionated.* When she first saw me with Dylan I could almost hear her matchmaking wheels turning."

"You seem happy."

"I am," Shelby said. "Don't get me wrong, I adore my husband and my kids and I'm thankful every day for them, but Rose started pushing the two of us together during the most terrifying time in my life."

"I wish I remembered more of my life."

Shelby reached out and patted Kresley on the knee. It was a very kind, very sisterly action. "I'm sorry there's nothing more I can do to help you. I've seen Matt and Gabe with their heads together, I'm sure they're doing everything possible. My husband is off on assignment again but I can get word to him if you'd like. Maybe an ATF agent would—"

"No," Kresley said quickly. So quickly that it was definitely rude. "I mean thank you, but I'm already indebted to you and Rose and Matt and Gabe and Susan."

"There's worse things in life than having to depend on friends," Shelby said. "Do you have any family?"

Kresley shook her head. "Only child of two only children."

Shelby offered a sympathetic smile. "It's hard not having family. My mother passed away when I was in my early twenties. I often think about how much she'd enjoy seeing my children. She'd have been a wonderful grandmother."

"Really?"

"Oh yes," Shelby said with a smile. "Would have spoiled Chad. Especially when it was just the two of us."

"Excuse me?"

"No, excuse me. It's common knowledge around here so I just naturally assume that everyone knows I kind of did things out of order. Chad was nine months old when Dylan and I got married."

"I can't imagine being a single parent."

"You work it out and learn to function on very little sleep," Shelby said with a sigh. "At the time I can remember wishing I was from a big family. You know, so I'd have some help. Dylan's one of six children. I love when they come to visit. You just can't ever have too many people to love in your life, can you?"

"I'm not sure I know," Kresley mused. The idea of family was really abstract without a memory.

"I don't know what's gotten into me," Shelby said with a shake of her head. "I'm not normally so insensitive."

"You're not being insensitive," Kresley said. "I'm assuming I'm your first and last amnesiac."

"I'm so sorry for you. I should go back," Shelby said, standing. "Maybe you could come over tomorrow for coffee or something?"

"That would definitely be inviting trouble. I'm on someone's hit list and I'm terrified I'm putting everyone around me in danger."

"No one can get back here without passing the video cameras. Believe me, Gabe rigged this place with motion detectors and all sorts of complicated security. Some company watches the video feed 24/7. I think the Rose Tattoo is as well protected as the Mona Lisa."

"That's good to know," Kresley said.

"It is and it isn't. There are monitors in the offices. How else did you think Rose and I knew you were here alone?"

"The soup and the biscuits are appreciated."

Shelby smiled. "Rose will be relentless, just so you know."

"Why would she think that Matt and I, well, that, we, um…"

"Susan has her crystals, Rose has her matchmaking. I said this place was safe, not normal. Besides, Rose is right, I think."

"About what?"

Shelby's eyes sparkled. "You and Matt."

"There is no me and Matt," Kresley insisted.

"Give it time," Shelby said as she reached for the deadbolt. "I enjoyed our little visit. And just overlook Rose's meddling."

"I can do that," Kresley promised.

Kresley locked herself in the apartment again and lifted the pot of soup to carry it into the kitchen. She wondered what was taking Matt so long. Sighing, she picked up the television remote and began to flip through the channels. Her jaw dropped when she saw her face plastered on the screen.

"... Kresley Judith Hayes. Surveillance tapes have led police to designate her as a person of interest in the shooting death of designer and Charleston native, Umberto Gianni. Anyone knowing the whereabouts of Kresley Hayes is asked to call Crime Stoppers at the number on the screen or you can contact the Charleston police directly at 843-..."

Chapter Ten

"My face is plastered all over the television," Kresley argued as she got into the passenger's seat of Gabe's Mercedes. After fastening her seatbelt, she slumped down, in no real hurry to get them arrested.

"The windows are tinted," Matt said, slightly amused.

Kresley relaxed a little. "What took you so long?"

"Gabe called about the credit card number used to buy your dress."

"And?"

"It belongs to Declan Callaghan." Matt read from a slip of paper he pulled out of the cup holder on the console. "And Gabe got a few hits on the license-plate numbers."

"Hits?"

"One guy in violation of his parole on a B and E and another guy with a bench warrant out. Ring any bells?" He handed her the paper.

"Sorry," she said as she scanned the names.

"Our bench-warrant guy is a Jamaican national,

Reginald Fox, aka Reggie Fox, aka Roman Fox, aka Foxy R failed to appear for a court date on a weapons charge.

"His last arrest, the one he'd skipped on, was for sale and possession of cocaine with a weapons charge tacked on."

"Sounds like a lovely man."

"Gets better," Matt said. "Foxy R's weapon of choice is a .45."

"How does that help us?"

"The cops pulled a .45 slug out of the wall of the T-shirt shop. Three guesses what kind of car Foxy R drives?"

"Black SUV?"

"Yep. Fully tricked out with tinted windows. All we have to do now is find the connection between Foxy R and the *Carolina Moon*."

"Don't people like that have to wait in jail until their trials?" she asked.

"Usually. But he got released on recognizance. Somehow this has to be tied to what Janice was investigating. The harbor patrol grabbed him up with ten kilos of cocaine and an assault rifle. Then the judge releases him on his own recognizance? Doesn't make any sense.

"If I find out who Foxy has in his pocket, I might get a little closer to finding Janice."

She glanced his way for a second, her eyes bright with determination. "I should turn myself in. With this kind of publicity, it isn't like anyone could do anything to me."

"Unfortunately, they can," Matt said. "No, you're safer at my place."

"Won't the police be at my apartment?"

"Perhaps."

"Then what do I do? And how can I go to the market at six? My face is everywhere."

"We'll figure that out."

The first thing she noticed was that her apartment door was ajar. The tickle of discomfort turned into a wave of anxiety when Matt reached over and unlocked the glove box in his car. He pulled his gun out and slid the top part to chamber a bullet.

"What are you doing?" Kresley asked. "The police could be in here. Or watching. Or it could be the guy who shot Gianni. Let's just go back to Charleston, please?"

Completely ignoring her, he said, "Stay here."

"No, thank you. My odds are better if I go where the gun goes."

Matt didn't seem to like her reply, but she didn't much care. She'd rather go inside and risk being face-to-face with a cop or a robber than be a sitting duck in her own parking lot.

"Stay behind me," Matt said.

They approached the apartment from the right; Matt held the weapon at his side until they got to the door. In a sudden move, he jumped into the doorway, the gun raised. He swept the room after kicking the door open.

Terrified, she followed in his wake, stepping over cushions, lamps and other debris. Matt checked the bedrooms and bathrooms, then the kitchen and the dining room. He stuffed the gun into the waistband of his jeans and said, "All clear."

"All trashed," Kresley remarked as she surveyed the apartment. The front doorknob was missing and the deadbolt had been drilled. The living-room sofa was sliced from arm to arm, as were the matching chairs. Every door and drawer in the entertainment center was open, the contents dumped on the floor next to the disemboweled cushions. The bedrooms and bathrooms were similarly destroyed.

"I'll watch the door. You've got two minutes to pack and then we're out of here."

Walking down the short hallway to the first bedroom, she found the mattresses on the twin beds sliced, one leaning against the wall. All the dresser drawers were empty, their contents scattered across the room.

Kresley got a whiff of perfume and instantly a morbid picture flashed in her brain.

Blood. Lots and lots of blood.

Kresley leaned against the wall until the dizziness passed.

When he saw that she was about to keel over, Matt fashioned a seat out of the sliced cushions. "Okay now?" he asked.

He crouched on his haunches, so they were eye-level. He was close enough that his minty breath washed over her face.

The instant he looked into her eyes, Matt felt a jolt in his gut. Okay, south of his gut. Wrong, inappropriate and impossible to ignore. The woman had no memory, a hole in her armpit from a .22, and several stitches in her hand from defensive knife wounds. Still, he couldn't stop himself. The emotion in her expression was a blend of vulnerability and strength.

"I'm fine," she said as she stood. "Just a flash of blood. Made me a little sick."

Matt tamped down the lust fogging his brain and refocused on the situation at hand. "What freaked you out?"

"The smell of perfume." she said as she grabbed a suitcase from among the debris and started shoving in clothing and shoes. She had to depend on the tags to know which had belonged to her roommates. Then she went into the bathroom, opened the medicine chest and almost frenetically examined the contents and made selections to add to the suitcase. Kresley opened a square pink bottle of perfume and did a little spritz into the air.

She swayed and the color drained from her face. Matt looped an arm around her waist as he pulled her against him so that her back was against his front. In the mirror, he watched her struggle to retain her composure. "What's with the perfume?" he asked when he saw her cheeks turn slightly pink.

"When I smell it I see blood. Pooled on the deck. Splattered on the walls."

"Is it your perfume?"

She looked up and met his gaze in the mirror. "I don't know. I don't think so."

"Close your eyes," Matt said.

"Why?"

"If you concentrate, then maybe you'll remember a detail that would help you flesh out the memory."

She shook her head. "I don't have time to remember right now. Let's just go before you get caught aiding and abetting me."

"It'll get better," Matt promised.

"Says who? What if I'm never able to fill in the blanks?

"You will. Just give it time."

"Did you go to medical school, too?" Kresley snapped.

"Kendall told me."

"What else did the doctor tell you?" she asked in a more reasoned tone. "Sorry I was snippy. I guess all this is just getting to me."

"You're forgiven, and Kendall said that you'd most likely get your memory slowly. Something about your mind protecting you from the trauma you witnessed."

"What do I do until then?"

"I think you're doing it," Matt said, taking the suitcase and leading her back toward the front door. "The amount of destruction tells me that whoever broke into the apartment didn't find whatever it was they hoped to find. So, either it, whatever *it* was, is still here or it had never been here in the first place."

In the car on the way back to his apartment, she said, "Really, Matt, I think the best course of action is for me to turn myself in to the police."

He kept his gaze straight ahead on the highway,

but she noticed a small vein at his temple throbbing and his jaw was taut. "No."

She raised her hands as she shrugged. "Why not?"

"How will you explain the last few days?"

"The truth. Don't worry—I'll leave your name out of it. I'll just tell them some very nice people helped me."

"You gonna include the truth that Kendall risked her job by removing a .22 slug from your body and not reporting it? She could lose her medical license."

"No. I won't say a word about Kendall."

"Or that Rose and Shelby gave you a place to stay. Particularly Shelby, since a felony conviction for aiding and abetting would probably cause her to lose her children.

"Or how about Gabe? He's been working night and day trying to help you— Hell, anyone at the Rose Tattoo who's seen you." He took a long, low breath. "Then there's me. I've helped you break several laws. If that becomes public, I can kiss my career at the FBI good-bye. Is that what you want, Kresley? Because one word to the authorities right now and you'll start a domino effect no one will be able to stop."

Her shoulders slumped and she looked down at her trembling hands. "Point taken. All the same, the police are looking for me. I can't stay with you, for all the same reasons you just enumerated."

"No one can connect you to the Rose Tattoo. It's better than some motel out on Highway 17," he said.

Kresley placed her hand on his bicep. "It would

be safer if I checked in to a motel. Some place random. I don't want you any more involved in this mess than you already are."

When they returned to his apartment, Matt shoved clothing from his dresser into a backpack. He spent less than a minute in the bathroom gathering his toiletries.

He had a laptop and some other equipment along with assorted cables. He stuffed those into a second backpack he took from the back of the broom closet.

She glanced at the clock in the kitchen. "What about the creepy guy who wants to meet me at the market at 6:00 p.m.?"

"Gabe's going to cover that while we relocate."

Kresley planted her good hand on her hip. "But he wants to meet *me*."

Matt hoisted the clothing backpack on his shoulder.

"Not going to happen. It's too dangerous now," Matt insisted.

"Think so?" she asked, grabbing a knife out of the kitchen drawer. "Come at me. I defended myself before, remember?"

Matt made a derisive little sound. "I'm not in the mood for games."

"Me, either," Kresley said holding the knife out for him. "Since we seem to be at an impasse, I'm proposing a tie breaker. You come at me with that knife and if I can't take it away from you, then I'll meekly follow whatever plan you come up with.

"You, meek?"

She ignored the dig. "But if I'm successful, we work out a plan for me to meet creepy guy at the market and then we go our separate ways."

He sighed heavily. "This is ridiculous. I've got more than a hundred pounds on you and FBI training."

"Then you don't have anything to lose, do you?"

"Yeah, I could break open your stitches or hurt your hand."

"If that happens, I promise not to blame you. Deal?"

"This is stupid," Matt said as he turned his back on her and went into the living room.

"You should have done it the easy way," Kresley said as she timed a front kick to catch him right behind the knee.

Matt was kneeling. Tossing the knife aside, Kresley came closer, planning a way to remove the backpack without actually hurting him. Suddenly, his leg shot out in an arc, literally slapping her feet out from under her. She fell on her tailbone. Hard.

Before she could recover, Matt was on top of her, straddling her at the waist, holding her hands above her head with his fingers wrapped around her wrists. "Motel it is," he said with a smug smile.

Kresley pressed against his grip, waiting for the right moment to use his own strength against him. Then suddenly she shot her foot high up on his thigh, half pushing, half rolling him up and over her.

Kresley stood, breathing heavily from the exertion. "Looks like the market wins."

Slowly, he got to his feet. "That wasn't fair. I was holding back because you're a girl and my mother told me never to hit girls."

Kresley scoffed. "You keep telling yourself that, DeMarco, if it makes you feel better about having your butt kicked by a girl."

"How about a compromise?"

"Such as?"

"You can meet the guy if, *if* Gabe and I won't be more than two feet away from you at all times. As adept as you are, you can't roundhouse-kick a bullet travelling at three thousand feet per second."

"Deal. Now what?"

"We've got enough time to check into a motel and get back in time for you to be at the market at six. I'll call Gabe from the car and fill him in. I'll also want him to find the safest place for you to stand."

"Sounds good to me." Kresley sucked in a deep breath, attempting to tamp down her uneasiness.

Matt drove out a dozen or so miles on Highway 17 toward Beauford.

"What's with the cooler?" Kresley asked, glancing into the back seat.

"Dinner."

"When did you have time to make dinner?"

"Not me, Rose and Shelby. They insisted."

"Mind if I look at Janice's file—the one you took from Gianni's place?"

"Be my guest," Matt said. "It's in the front zipper compartment in the blue-and-black backpack."

Kresley ran her fingers over the file, curious about

the contents. There were only four pages inside it—a receipt, an order form, a page of measurements and the bottom page was a digital photo.

With a burst of hot, white light, her mind immediately played a conversation with the woman in the photo. "I remember her being at Gianni's."

"Who? Janice?"

Kresley nodded as Matt jerked the Mercedes off to the shoulder and twisted to face her. "She helped me get dressed that night." Kresley struggled to hold on to the memory. "Is there a public bathroom near the dock where the *Carolina Moon* was moored?

"Yes. About a hundred yards from where the yacht was tied up when it was in port."

"She was in the restroom taping something to me and reminding me that I had to get him on tape."

"Him, who?"

"I don't know. There was someone else there, too."

"Who?"

Squeezing her eyes closed, Kresley tried to bring the shadowy figure into focus.

"He's thin and there's something weird about his hair."

"That's it?" Matt asked in a clipped tone.

Kresley glared at him. "It's not like I'm tuning into NPR here. Cut me some slack."

"Sorry," he said, punctuating his remark by placing his hand on her shoulder and giving a gentle squeeze.

His thumb ran along her collarbone, making it impossible for her to think. She pushed his hand away and said, "I can't concentrate when you touch me. I remember being terrified."

"Of?"

"She kept reminding me that I had to get him on tape. That if I didn't she couldn't build her case."

"Do you remember how she was dressed? Was she going aboard the yacht with you?"

"Can't remember, sorry."

"Then?"

Kresley's eyes remained closed. "Then it skips ahead. I'm on the boat. I can hear the water lapping against the fiberglass hull. I'm below deck. I've got my phone in my hand, I'm pressing keys, and then I looked out the porthole and..." She opened her eyes. "That's it."

Grasping her face in his hands, Matt kissed her. It was a quick action, or rather reaction. She'd felt none of the heat of his earlier kisses. "That's a lot."

After making a U-turn, Matt pulled into a two-level motel, or *otel* to be exact. The *M* was missing from the sign. The paint was peeling and the place stank because they were retarring the roof.

"This is the only option?" Kresley asked as she reached for the door handle.

"Sorry, the Ritz was booked," he replied dryly. "I want you to walk over there," he said, pointing toward the stairway. It went up a half flight, then there was a platform, then a second set of stairs to the upper floor's walkway. "Get close under the landing so you can't be seen while I register."

"I don't think I'm going to like being a fugitive."

Chapter Eleven

Since it was April, 6:00 p.m. was dusk—primo feeding time for the famous black mosquitoes in South Carolina.

The meeting place was a stretch of Market Street where everyone from local basket weavers to record dealers came to sell their wares in a three-block-long swap meet.

Via cell phone, Gabe had directed her to stand near the western exit but remain under a white canopy. The smell of food grilling mingled with the strong odor of floral extracts for sale in the booth directly to her right. Kresley thought of Susan and smiled. She'd probably find the collection of aromas magical.

The only magic Kresley was feeling was the miracle of not throwing up. Even though Matt was in her line of sight, as exposed as she was, she still felt extremely vulnerable. He was flipping through a collection of old movie posters, his face obscured by the ridiculously large-brimmed sea-grass hat he'd purchased at the first booth.

It was warm, so the soft breeze felt good against her perspiring skin. The light wind suddenly brought with it the smell of ripe vegetables, giving Kresley a sudden feeling of déjà vu.

In her mind's eye, she was standing next to a vile-smelling Dumpster behind a strip mall. It was dark, the only light a weak street lamp at the entrance to the narrow street. Nervously, she tapped her toe, the staccato sound a little too loud in the confines of the alley. Her heart rate increased when a big, black SUV pulled into the side street, coming to a stop so that she was parallel to the passenger's door. The window slid down, but she could only make out shadows.

"Everything's been arranged," a woman's voice said. "Allen will make sure none of the other women go near the bathroom. Meet me there at six-thirty."

"Who's Allen?"

"It's a romantic, sunset dinner cruise. If you don't have a date, you'll stick out like the proverbial sore thumb. Allen Cain is one of mine, he can be trusted. Call me as soon as you see the boat. Just Allen. Other than him, trust no one."

Then nothing. Kresley was so frustrated she wanted to scream. Her own mind was taunting her, teasing her with bits of this and chunks of that. Since she'd already recalled that there was a woman taping a recorder to her rib cage before the cruise, Kresley deduced the woman in the restroom and the woman in the black SUV were one and the same. As much as she wanted to close the three feet of space between her and Matt, she couldn't. Anything out of the ordinary would probably spook the creepy guy.

A woman, short with a few extra pounds on her small frame, pushed her stroller over Kresley's feet. Kresley winced.

"I'm so sorry," the woman insisted over and over as she pushed the stroller forward and locked the wheels so it wouldn't roll away. "Let me have a look."

"I'm fine," Kresley insisted.

"I used to be a nurse," the woman persisted, crouching down for a closer inspection of Kresley's feet.

Her light brown hair was shoulder length and gathered into a rubber band and she had small gold hoops in her ears. She was wearing cargo pants, running shoes and a sleeveless blouse. All looked new. Judging by her manicure, and the lack of calluses on her hands, she didn't do a lot of manual labor.

Standing, the woman pulled a notepad out of the bag hooked on the stroller's handle and wrote quickly. She folded it once, and then thrust it at Kresley. "It was *totally* my fault," she said. "I wrote down all my information. If later, you decide you need medical attention, just send the bills to my home."

"I'm fine," Kresley said for the umpteenth time. "Your baby's probably being eaten by the mosquitoes."

"Right," the brunette said as she went to the

stroller, unlocked the wheels, and pushed eastward through the crowd.

Kresley watched as the woman plowed through people. It looked more as if she was pushing a lawn mower than a baby carriage. Kresley's stomach fell when she read the time—six minutes after the hour. Crap, maybe the guy was spooked by kamikaze mommy.

She was about to toss the piece of paper, then saw what was written in block letters:

> Unless you want to die, get on the 212 bus. Sit two seats in front of the rear exit.

Quickly, she fashioned a paper airplane out of the note and sent it soaring toward Matt. Kresley's heart pounded so hard she thought for sure it would break through her chest at any second. So much for Matt and Gabe blending in.

He read the note, then nodded in the direction of the exit. They were parallel as they navigated out of the market.

She followed the same path as kamikaze mommy. Running whenever there was a break in the crowd. She found the stroller—with a doll in it—abandoned by a signpost. The woman had left it there for a reason. The sign pointed the way to the bus stop.

Trying to be nonchalant about it, she looked behind her just to make sure she wasn't alone. Kresley found Gabe and Matt stuck behind a group of tourists admiring a basket-weaving demonstration. There was no way they'd make it around the bottleneck in time to catch up with her.

Kresley continued walking slowly to the bus stop, arriving just as the bus belched out rank fumes and the hydraulics hissed. She stood at the curb too scared to move. Kresley was about to step back when she felt the cold barrel of a gun pressed at her back.

"Get on the bus." The voice against her ear was a garbled whisper. The words might have been difficult to hear but she wasn't the least bit confused about the gun. She had no doubt that if she didn't get on the bus, he'd shoot her then and there.

There were only three other people on the bus. Possibly more, but she didn't dare turn around. Not much comfort. This same person had killed at least six people on the yacht.

"Good," came the deep male voice she recognized from the phone calls. "You finally followed my instructions. My boss will be pleased."

The bus lurched and whooshed as it pulled away from the curb. Kresley balanced herself by using the railing on the seat in front of her. The creepy guy was right behind her. She could feel his warm breath crest over her shoulders. It was a revolting feeling.

"Did you bring it?"

"I don't know what *it* is," she hissed.

"No time to be cute," he said. "Hand it over."

"I really don't have it. When I washed up on the beach, I didn't have anything but my dress. Is that it? Is there something about the dress that—"

"I don't believe you, Kresley. You're a smart girl.

I'm sure you've figured everything out by now. What's up? Maybe you'd like a cut. Is that it? You're holding out for a piece of the action?"

"I'm holding out for a memory," she returned, trying her best not to cry. "I don't want a piece of anything. I just want to be left alone."

"I'm gonna do whatever it takes to get that tape back," he said in a harsh, angry whisper against her ear. "Or did you give it to him already? I couldn't find it in your apartment or in your car."

"That's because I'm telling the truth. I don't have anything and I don't remember anything. If I had what you wanted, believe me, I'd give it to you in a heartbeat."

"I'm feeling generous, Kresley. I'll give you twenty-four hours, then if I don't have it in my hands, I'm going to make you watch me kill your boyfriend, then I'll kill you. *Slowly.*"

A small ding sounded in the bus, and the vehicle pulled over. No one got off from the front exit, but she heard the back door open. It wasn't until the bus had started to move into traffic that she dared turn around. The seat was empty.

Standing, Kresley raced to the rear of the bus and looked back at the bus stop. There were three men in the area. One was twentyish; the one with his back to her had a medium build and maybe he was balding; the last one was large and his muscles were about six times the size of normal. If she had to guess, she'd bet Mister Steroid was the creepy guy.

Getting off at the next stop and following the bus

driver's instructions, Kresley walked across the street to the bus stop and waited for the next bus back to the market.

About three minutes later, the green Mercedes pulled to a screeching halt in the center of the street. Matt got out of the passenger's seat. He did not look pleased. Well, too darn bad. She put up her hand as she walked toward him. "Before you ream me…"

In a matter of seconds, Matt was kissing her, and then she was lifted off the ground and spun around. After some time, he put her down, his expression a blend of relief and anger. She assumed Gabe was behind the wheel.

"What were you thinking?"

Ignoring his question, Kresley filled him in on the latest snippet of memory. "I met her more than once."

"Are you sure it was Janice?"

"I'm sure the woman's voice in the SUV was the same as the woman who had me wearing that tape recorder. Oh, and the guy making the calls has a boss."

Matt steered Kresley toward Gabe, then to the car. Matt and Gabe ran possibilities while they drove back to the parking lot where Matt's Jeep was parked. The blood was still cruising through Kresley's veins at warp speed. She wondered how people with dangerous jobs handled the rush of adrenaline and overwhelming fear. She was a jittery blob.

"Call me if you need anything," Gabe said.

"Let's move," Matt started the Jeep's engine. "The

longer we're out in public, the more likely it is that you'll be recognized. If that happens, the cops will be all over you."

"Thanks for that cheery thought. I can't swear to it, but I think Mister Steroid was the guy who slaughtered everyone on the yacht."

"Was it his voice? The way he moved?"

"It's more like an impression. No pun intended but if he was the muscle, then who is pulling his strings and why?" Kresley placed her hand on her forehead and squeezed. As if one good squish would make the memories come back. "Okay, if I was supposed to get *him* on tape, that limits the possibilities, right?"

"Yeah," Matt agreed. "There were four men on the yacht that night. Jason Wellington and Tom Gibson's bodies have been claimed by their families. Two John Does are at the morgue. Their bodies washed up on shore but we think they're from the yacht."

"Try Allen Cain. The woman told me he was one of hers. If the woman was Janice that would make him another FBI agent working undercover, right? Or maybe someone from the Charleston police helping her out?"

Matt shook his head. "If that were true, his fingerprints would be in the system. All law-enforcement agencies keep reference prints on their agents and officers. Helps rule them out at crime scenes."

"You said she liked to cut corners, so maybe this Cain guy was like me, an innocent bystander who got caught up in...in *something*."

"As soon as we get to the motel, we'll see if we can find his driver's license photo."

If she could identify the people on the yacht, maybe that would lead her to Mister Steroid's boss.

The small motel room, furnished in seventies' style, matted shag carpet and all, had two double beds. Everything was some shade of brown or rust polyester. There was a window air-conditioner that spewed a moldy, musty smell and dripped condensation on a soggy circle of carpeting beneath the window.

The bathroom was small with avocado tiles, sink and tub. Kresley was no decorator but she didn't think the grout between the tiles was supposed to be black. "Forget threatening phone calls, we're going to die from exposure to toxic mold."

"I've seen worse, we'll live," he called out to her.

She returned to the bedroom to find the contents of the his red backpack laid out on one bed. "That's very high-tech."

"Yes, it is," Matt agreed, attaching the last of the power cords. "The machine has its own phone built in. All I have to do," he said as his large fingers pecked away at the keyboard, "is connect to the FBI database."

"Not exactly something you can get at Best Buy, huh?"

"I'm going to use Janice's log-in, just in case."

"In case of what?"

The hard drive made a spinning sound, and then the emblem of the FBI filled the screen. Matt typed only with his forefingers, and even then managed to make several typos.

"Move," she said impatiently.

Matt slid over on the bed, giving her the spot he'd occupied.

Kresley typed *Allen Cain* into the name search. The screen rolled at warp speed, names spinning so fast it made her dizzy to watch.

Then it stopped and pinged. Eyes Only. Enter Password to Continue. "That can't be good," Kresley muttered. She typed the name in again, only this time she substituted an *a* for the *e* in Allan. No Records Found. Finally, she tried *Alan* with the same result. She did variations on *Cain, Kane, Cane,* etc., nothing worked. "I'm open to suggestions."

"Try your name."

As she typed, she talked. "I can't have an FBI fi— What?"

Eyes Only. Enter Password to Continue. "I *can* have an FBI file. Why? I'm not that important. And why is it 'eyes only'?"

"Agents use that to protect the identities of CIs."

"CIs?"

"Confidential informants."

"Do you know the password?"

Frustrated, Matt shook his head. Pulling the cooler between the two beds, he got a towel from the bath and used it as a tablecloth after he'd taken out all the containers, plates and utensils.

Shelby or Rose had also thought to put in a bottle of wine and two glasses. "Yum," Kresley remarked when she smelled fried chicken, potato salad and coleslaw. There were also two generous slices of—if her nose wasn't playing tricks on her—lemon pound cake. Matt sat on one bed, Kresley took the other. Placing a napkin in her lap, she put the chicken on a plate while Matt scooped the salads onto their plates.

"Sweet tea or wine?" he asked.

"Wine. It's been a long day."

He was openly staring at her. It went on for several minutes before he said, "You're an amazing woman."

Heat burned on Kresley's cheeks. "With big chunks of her memory missing." She was trying to deflect the praise, not sure she could keep her emotions in check when he complimented her.

"But it hasn't freaked you out."

"Sure it has," she said, after swallowing the best fried chicken she'd ever put in her mouth. "This is *really* good."

"How?"

"I think it's in the batter. That's what sets it apart from other fried chicken I've had."

Matt laughed softly. "I didn't mean how is the chicken batter, though DeLancey will be thrilled to hear that. If all this is freaking you out, you're hiding it well."

Kresley sampled the salads; both were excellent. It was a little awkward eating with her right hand. "I know this is going to sound really weird but I think I'm almost afraid of getting my memory back."

"You're right, it does sound weird," Matt refilled

her wineglass. "What's the last concrete memory you have?"

"Forgetting the snippets?"

"Yes."

Putting her fork down, Kresley ran her finger around the rim of her glass. "I don't remember being a kid or a teenager or even college. The closest thing I have to a past is being at the apartment, at the kitchen table trying to decide which courses to take. The quarter started April fifth so it had to have been before then."

"Where were your roommates?"

"Out."

"Doing what?"

"On dates, I guess. Remember, I told you we weren't exactly on the best of terms. So I doubt they would have brought me into their confidence."

"Do you remember them going out in Gianni dresses?"

Kresley nodded. "I think so. Maybe. Or I'm just remembering what Gabe said and treating it like a memory. I didn't know they were Gianni, just that they weren't off the rack from T.J. Maxx. They'd go out every six weeks or so."

"They never invited you?"

"Abby did one night when Emma was sick."

"Did you go?"

She shook her head. "I don't remember. Sorry."

"You're not much of a romantic, are you?"

"I guess not. And before you ask, I have no idea if I had a good or bad childhood."

He smiled. "If it was anything like mine, being

shuffled from one foster home to the next, that would be a gift."

"Why were you in foster care?" she asked, then apologized. "That's none of my business. Sorry."

"It's no great secret. My mother loved me, just not as much as she loved Jack Daniel's."

That little indefinable expression passed across his face before the sexy smile with those incredible dimples appeared and made her heart skip several beats. He wiped his hands, and then put away the small amount of food left.

Kresley relaxed, arranged pillows behind her and sipped more wine.

Matt slid up beside her. Lifting several strands of her hair, he watched as it slipped through his fingers. "You have beautiful hair. Like silk."

"Thank you," Kresley's body temperature shot up about ten degrees.

Moving her hair out of the way, Matt kissed her neck, teasing her with the tip of his tongue.

His lips brushed against the sensitive skin just below her earlobe. The feel of his gentle kisses drew her stomach into a knot of anticipation. Closing her eyes, she concentrated on the glorious sensations. His grip tightened as his tongue traced a path up to her ear. Her breath caught when he teasingly nibbled the edge of her lobe.

His hands traveled upward and rested against her rib cage. She was aware of everything—his fingers, the feel of his solid body molded against hers, the intoxicating kisses.

"You smell wonderful," he said against her heated skin.

"Matt," she whispered his name.

His mouth stilled and he gripped her waist, turning her in his arms. His eyes were thickly lashed and hooded. A lock of his jet-black hair had fallen forward and rested just above his brows. His chiseled mouth was curved in an effortlessly sexy half smile.

"I've kept my hands off you for days," he said. He applied pressure to the middle of her back, urging her closer to him.

"Should I call the Guinness World Record people?" she managed to joke above her rapid heartbeat.

"It was a mutual thing and you know it. We've done a good job at pretending this wasn't between us," he continued, punctuating his remark with a kiss on her forehead. "I can't tell you how often I've looked at you and thought of nothing but this."

His palms slid up her back and across her shoulders until he cradled her face in his hands. Matt tilted her head back and hesitated only fractionally before his mouth found hers. Instinctively, Kresley's hand went to his waist.

The scent of soap and cologne filled her nostrils as the exquisite pressure of his mouth increased. Her mind was no longer capable of rational thought. All her attention was honed on the intense sensations filling her with fierce desire.

She reveled in the feel of his strong body against hers. As he deepened the kiss into something more demanding, she succumbed to the potent dose of longing.

She began to explore the solid contours of his body beneath his T-shirt. Everywhere she touched, she was aware of the distinct outline of corded muscle.

When he lifted his head, his eyes met hers and he quietly studied her face. His breaths were coming in short, almost raspy gulps and she watched the tiny vein at his temple race in time with her own rapid heartbeat.

His next kiss lasted for several heavenly moments.

Until someone started pounding on the door.

"Police! Open the door!"

Chapter Twelve

"Hang on! Be right there," Matt called as he shoved the few things Kresley had unpacked back into her bag. After a quick check out the back window, he dropped the suitcase into the walkway behind the motel.

As he pulled his shirt off, he said, "Go. I'll meet you at the burger joint across the field as soon as I get rid of the cops."

Impatient pounding reverberated through the small room as Matt started to unzip his pants. That alone was enough to propel Kresley out the window and through the dense vegetation.

After turning the shower on full blast, he stepped into it just long enough to saturate his hair, then got out and secured a thin, whitish towel around his waist.

The pounding got louder. "Be there in a minute!" he shouted, and then spotted the two glasses on the nightstand. Pouring the contents of one into the other, he shoved the empty glass under the pillow, then went to the door and yanked it open. "Yes?"

The two officers were a study in contrasts. One was older, fifties or so, with a beer gut and mustard on his tie. Officer number two was tall, skinny and definitely a rookie. Only a newbie would unhook his holster without just cause.

"We received a tip that Kresley Hayes is staying here with you."

Matt laughed. "Your tip was wrong. As you can see, I'm all alone."

"Mind if we come in?"

"Not at all," Matt answered, holding the door open wider. "There's just this room and a bath."

The younger officer went into the bathroom, while the older one struggled to get down on one knee to check under the beds. It took him twice as long to hoist himself off the floor. He didn't know it but his hand was mere inches from the glass Matt had secreted away.

"Window's open," the newbie reported.

"As far as I know that isn't a felony. I was trying not to fog up the mirror," Matt explained. "Besides, you'd have to be one tiny person to squeeze through that thing."

"You have an apartment in town, correct?" the older one asked.

"Yes."

"So you're out here because…"

"Ever live twenty feet from your job?" Matt said with a shake of his head and a roll of his eyes. "I just came out to get away and do some shrimping." He pointed to the cooler. "With any luck, tomorrow it'll be full of shrimp."

"You haven't seen Kresley Hayes?"

"I saw her on the news." That was true.

"Know any reason why someone would call the tip line, identify you and give us this location?"

"Scorned girlfriend, maybe? I didn't exactly keep it a secret that I was going shrimping today."

"Anyone who can confirm that?"

"Gabe Langston."

They seemed satisfied with his answers and left. Matt peeked through the dusty draperies and watched as they got into their patrol car.

Retrieving his phone, he called Gabe and gave him the heads-up. "How would anyone know where we were?" he asked. "I picked this motel randomly."

"Make any calls?"

"Nope. And neither did Kresley."

"Yeah, I know. I have the clone, remember. You should be careful, Matt. She took one hell of a chance this evening and my take is the only reason she put herself in harm's way was because of you."

"It isn't like that, Gabe. Kendall told me that Kresley would probably latch on to me until she gets her memory back. Then I'm sure she'll go back to her life."

"Is that disappointment I hear in your tone?"

No. Yes. Maybe. "Not sure." He began to pace the small confines of the motel room. "What are we missing?"

"Tell me everything you did."

Matt thought for a few minutes, then gave a detailed account of their activities, stopping short of telling Gabe if the cops hadn't come to the door, they would probably have had sex. No, not probably. Definitely. Matt felt like a teenager, eager and unable to control his physical response to Kresley. What kind of a man lusts after a woman who's neck-deep in trouble?

"My guess is someone traced back your IP address."

"But I logged in as Janice."

"And your someone must have flagged Janice's account for activity."

"How sophisticated would the person have to be?"

"If the person knew the account information, any motivated twelve-year-old could triangulate and do a trace. The cops just pulled up."

"Thanks, Gabe."

"You'd do the same for me."

Matt got dressed, and then checked the parking lot for unmarked cars. Easy to spot—two occupants sipping coffee or reading newspapers. Stakeouts were boring as hell.

Unlike Kresley, he couldn't squeeze through the window. He left the same way he'd come in—through the front door. He tossed his backpacks and the cooler into the Jeep and drove to the burger place.

When he didn't see her, panic ran roughshod over every other emotion. The tires squealed as he came to an abrupt halt. So abrupt that he left skid marks and the acrid stench of burned rubber filled the air.

Maybe she was staying out of sight in the ladies'

room. His palms were sweating when he went to open the door.

"Pssssst!"

Matt turned to see Kresley clutching her suitcase, tucked in the shadows on the side of the building. He walked over and instinctively placed an arm around her shoulder. "Hurt anything when you were climbing out of that window?"

"No harm done. What did the police say? How did they know we were together?"

"All good questions that I will answer as soon as we get out on the road."

No sooner had Matt started back up Highway 17 toward Charleston than Kresley's cell phone rang. She put it on speaker. "Hello?"

"Close call back at the motel, wasn't it?"

"Yes."

"Lucky you were on the first floor," Creepy phone guy said.

"Look, I know you think I have something but I don't. Anything that was taped to me had to have fallen off while I was trying not to drown."

"Is it more money? Is that what you're holding out for?"

Matt mouthed, "Keep him talking." Then he dialed a number on his own phone and murmured something Kresley couldn't hear.

"No. Money doesn't motivate me. What else do you have? And how does helping the police find me help you?" Kresley asked, hoping to draw out some information, anything that could be useful.

"That was my boss's call. I'll call you tomorrow, Kresley. You and Matt have sweet dreams."

Kresley's call ended, but Matt's continued for a couple of more minutes.

"Really?" she heard him say. "Think you can get her to agree? Great." Then a pause, and "No, we'll deal with it tonight."

"What are we dealing with tonight?" she asked.

"Feel up to going back on the yacht?"

The mere thought of going back there gave her goose bumps. "What if someone recognizes me?"

"It's dark," Matt said. "That always helps. We're going to swing by my apartment on our way to the yacht.

"Gabe made a second clone of your cell phone. He can listen in, and triangulate off the cell towers."

"In plain English, please?"

"Based on which towers the signal hit, he narrowed the location to inside the Coast Guard station."

Kresley's heart skipped a beat. "I *knew* I saw a rescue boat that night."

"I know. So it looks like some of this is an inside job."

"Only we still don't know what *it* is."

"That's why we're going to the yacht. Maybe being back on board will shake something loose. I know Kendall said I shouldn't push, but the last few times you've recovered hunks of memory, it has been triggered by sights or smells."

Matt checked his mirrors constantly, and in a

practiced sweep to be sure no one was following them. She imagined it was harder to tail a vehicle at night, when one set of back lights must look pretty much like a hundred others. She appreciated his vigilance. Still, she felt as though they had a target painted on them as Matt drove through the dark back streets and darker alleys toward the marina.

Since everything near the marina was closed, there were only a few cars parked in the lot. "Where's my car?" she asked, recalling Gabe or Matt having said her lime-green VW had been in the lot.

"Towed," Matt said. "The cops took it to their lab."

"For what?"

"To see if there's any evidence. It's standard procedure," he assured her. "You won't be too pleased when they return it."

"Because?"

"Because they will have taken it apart and the whole thing will be covered in fingerprint dust."

"Don't they have to clean it up?"

He offered a wry smile. "They're cops, not body-shop mechanics."

"That sucks."

"Ready?" he asked.

No. "Sure."

The yacht was secured at the end of the dock. It was the only boat there. There was only one light source, a streetlamp illuminating the boardwalk.

Kresley felt her pulse rate climb as she neared the yacht. She grabbed Matt's arm. "Is it still bloody?"

"Nope, the owner hired a clean-up crew as soon

as the Coast Guard and the cops released it back to him. By the way, your earring was found under one of the bodies."

"That's why they're so interested in me."

"Yep."

She glanced up at his handsome profile. "How come you believe me? You've believed me from the very beginning."

"Your wounds are inconsistent with you being the attacker."

"When I think about that night, I hear Janice's voice on the boat, only the images in my head tell me she wasn't on the boat. The last time I saw her was in that restroom," she said pointing back toward the cinder-block building they'd just passed. "Everyone on the yacht was dressed to the nines. Janice was in jeans and a top."

They parked near the boat at the gate of a home with a For Sale sign stuck in the tall grass of its front lawn.

"Are you sure you can do this?" he asked her.

"No, but nothing ventured, nothing gained."

The minute she stepped on the polished teak decking and smelled the briny, diesel-tainted water, images came at her fast and furiously. As if someone had hit the rewind button, she began reliving the attack. She was down below, looking out the porthole. It was dark, so all she could really make out was the silhouette of a boat coming toward them. Intuition told her to lift her cell phone and take a picture of the approaching boat.

She reached for her phone, took the picture, and then dialed the number she'd been given by Janice, she was almost sure. A man answered but quickly put Janice on the line. The connection was terrible, as if someone was standing behind a jet engine.

"You have to get him on tape," she reiterated. "I need to hear it in his own voice."

"I can barely hear you. What should I do?"

"Take pictures of the cocaine on the boat and e-mail them to me."

"Okay."

"Then get above deck and get close enough to him so the recorder can pick up his voice."

"Anything else?"

"Yeah, don't get caught."

Kresley recalled a sick feeling in her stomach, but she went past the captain's cabin to the sliding doors that led to the hold. Packages that looked a lot like fluffy pillows were stacked in the hold. As instructed, Kresley took pictures with her cell phone, hoping there was sufficient light to make the pictures clear enough.

Then as discreetly as possible, she went upstairs.

Matt held her shivering body close against his as she related what she was remembering.

"My hands were shaking and I was trying to e-mail the pictures but I kept dialing the wrong number. I remember thinking I should have written it down before erasing it."

"Erasing it from where?" Matt asked.

"The board."

"What board?"

"There was a message board on the back of my bedroom door. Janice wrote down the phone number and had me recite it over and over night after night in preparation for the cruise."

"Are you sure it was her?"

"It was definitely Janice."

"Can you still see the number?"

She shook her head. "No. I panicked as I climbed the stairs. I remember thinking she'd be furious with me so I highlighted the photos and e-mailed them to the online locker where I keep my assignments and important stuff I can't afford to lose."

"There was no history of accessing an online locker on the laptop we found at your apartment."

"That wasn't my laptop," Kresley said. "Mine was older, bigger and heavier. The one in the apartment was nearly new and sleek. It must have belonged to one of my other roommates."

"Or Janice planted it. There were password-protected subfolders for you and all your roommates."

"Why would she do that?"

"Misdirection. If nothing else, the Charleston PD will send it to their techies for analysis. I'm sure they'll find something incriminating about one or all of you."

"That's encouraging," Kresley groaned as she carefully navigated the angled ramp. Matt was close behind. "Have you considered…"

"Considered what?" he asked, his voice barely above a whisper as they moved through the shadows.

"There are other possibilities."

"Janice being dead?" he asked in a flat tone.

"Yes. Or maybe she isn't the person you think she is."

Matt was quiet until he slipped behind the wheel of the Jeep.

The night air was cooler and carried the scent of roses from the arbor beyond the iron gate of the vacant home. "So what now?" she asked. "I can use your laptop and retrieve the pictures," she suggested.

Matt shook his head. "I think that's how they found us at the motel. My laptop has its own phone line built in. If you know what to look for, you can triangulate its signal just like a cell phone."

"Who would know that?"

"A hacker."

"And?" she pressed.

"Agents and upper-level civilian employees of the FBI."

Kresley placed her hand on his forearm. "Everything is starting to point in one direction," she said gently.

In the dim light from the dashboard, she saw Matt's grip on the steering wheel tighten. Then he shook his head. "I've known Janice for years."

"People change."

"And you know this how? You can't even remember your own phone number."

Chapter Thirteen

They spent the night at Matt's apartment. Like warring factions, Matt went into one bedroom while Kresley took the other. They barely spoke. She understood Matt's reluctance to so much as consider Janice might be deeply involved in drug smuggling and worse, far worse, that bloody massacre on the yacht.

Well, Kresley had her own agenda. Staying alive. If that meant alienating Matt, so be it. She rose first, dressed in jeans and a white T-shirt, then went to make coffee. The percolator gurgled for the final time as Matt emerged from his bedroom.

"Good morning," she said cautiously.

"Morning," He stood next to her as she poured coffee into the mug she'd found in the cabinet. "Sleep well?"

"Yes. Knowing the Rose Tattoo's security system would warn me if the police showed up let me relax. You?"

He rubbed his hands over his face and his eyes

were slightly bloodshot. "I'm fine." As he reached above her to get a coffee cup, his bare torso bumped her. "Sorry," he mumbled.

When he joined her at the table, his opinion of her coffee was about as enthusiastic as hers was of his. "Any weaker and it would be hot water."

"This is your apartment. Dump it out and make another pot."

"It's fine."

"Is everything going to be 'fine' today?" she asked after a long, poignant silence.

He shook his head.

His hair was mussed and he had a shadow of a beard. Even though he was being a stubborn jerk, he was an attractive stubborn jerk.

"Going somewhere?" he asked.

"I looked in the Yellow Pages and there's an Internet café not far from here."

"Going out in public is risky. If the cops don't get you, there's still the guy from the bus."

"Maybe the photos—or something in them—are what he wants. If so, I can take care of all my problems. I give him a set and then I give the police a set. Everyone walks away happy."

"Assuming you walk away," Matt said.

"If you've got a better idea, I'm all ears."

He didn't, so an hour later, they left for the café.

The placed smelled of rich coffee and freshly baked croissants, muffins and other pastries. Matt took out his wallet and handed her a credit card. At first she was confused, then Kresley saw the slot off to the left of the bolted-down computer in one of the partitioned cubicles. Matt went for coffee and muffins while she paid twenty-five dollars for the privilege of logging on.

Scrolling through the documents and photographs, she finally found the e-mail she'd sent from her phone. There were three uploads with attachments. She clicked the first one. It was grainy and dark, but there was no mistaking the plastic-wrapped bricks of cocaine.

"That's a lot of blow." Matt whistled as he placed two extra-large coffees and two blueberry muffins next to her, then rolled a chair over so he was just behind and to the right of her. Using just one hand, she managed to command the machine to print out two copies.

"You're better one-handed than I am with both," Matt remarked, his breath tickling her neck. With her hair hastily twisted up, her neck was bare. The skin was sensitive, overly so if this was all it took to distract her.

"Gonna click the next file open any time soon?"

"Clicking," she said, wincing when her voice came out in a libidinous squeak. The second photo was not just grainy; it focused on the porthole and not the image in the distance. She sent this one to the printer, as well.

"I'm not sure that one was worth printing."

"We'll see," she said, fidgeting in the seat each time his arm brushed hers. And it happened a lot. Too often to be accidental. "That isn't helping."

"Really?" he asked and she could hear amusement in his tone. Using just one finger, he slowly drew it upward. Over her wrist, then her forearm, then all the way to her shoulder. "I'm just trying to apologize for being testy."

Kresley tingled all over. Her skin was on fire and her insides had turned into molten mush. "You weren't testy, you were sulky."

"Sorry," he said close to her ear.

She'd given up on trying to maintain normal breathing, now she was just struggling to keep from moaning. "Enjoying yourself?"

"Immensely," he answered as his finger traveled to her earlobe. "You?"

"Sure. If I wasn't wanted for murder, I'd be all over you."

The last file wasn't a photo, it was a video. One taken from a low angle, most likely because Kresley'd had the phone palmed in her hand and didn't want anyone to know she was taking photos.

"Look at this," Kresley said, distracted by her lust.

She recognized her roommates, even Emma who had her back to the lens. She counted four men and, including herself, four women. It seemed as if every time one of the unknown males was about to come into view, someone would move, blocking her shot. There was one quick glimpse of one of the unknowns. She played the last few seconds of video, which consisted of a blond guy handing her a flute of champagne and telling her it was time to go to the port side for the show. "Does the guy in the background have white hair or is that a captain's hat?" Kresley asked as she squinted and replayed the video over and over.

"Can't tell. My laptop has a program that would let us go frame by frame but we can't risk using it."

"We can if we're mobile, right?"

"Right." Matt kissed her forehead. "I like the way you think."

She went over to the pictures then scanned them into a larger machine with photo-enhancing software. She cleared enough of the graininess so the image of the cocaine was clear. The other photo, the one of Emma and Jason and Abby with Tom weren't much help in identifying the John Does stuck in limbo in the morgue. She bought a disc, then burned a DVD of the video clip, careful not to make eye contact with the clerk. The last thing she needed was to be identified and taken in for questioning by the police before she had a chance to really look at what she'd literally risked her life to get.

All the while, she felt as if everyone was just seconds away from calling Crime Stoppers.

They took the Jeep to the Battery and drove in circles, past the Civil War cannons lining Charleston Harbor. The air was sweet with Confederate jasmine and since the sun was up, it was difficult to see the laptop screen. Matt kept checking his watch.

Thanks to a fender bender, they were stuck at a traffic light near the Citadel for several minutes. Then to her absolute mortification, she looked ahead and saw no fewer than three patrol cars in and around the intersection.

"What do we do?" she asked in a near-whisper.

"There's a baseball cap in the back. Close the laptop and put it on."

They were only five cars from rolling right past a policeman. "A baseball cap? That's your solution?"

"It will work."

Kresley's heart pounded like crazy as they rolled through the intersection. One patrolman was close enough that she literally could have reached over and touched him. He seemed more interested in keeping the traffic moving.

Her hands were shaking long after they'd cleared the traffic jam. "I don't have the nerve to be an agent," she said as she let out the breath she'd been holding.

"You're doing fine. Keep working on that video."

Matt drove, watched the road and continually checked out the back window. At first Kresley thought he was just being super vigilant. But he didn't respond when she said his name.

"Matt?" she said louder while jabbing him with an elbow. "I'm slowly making progress. We have a problem. The battery may not last long enough to continue cleaning the video. Any chance you have some fancy agent gadget that will buy some time?"

"Hang on a second," he said, his gaze split between the rearview mirror and the roadway ahead.

Hearing something odd in his tone, she asked, "What is it?"

"Maybe nothing."

Kresley started to looked back over her shoulder.

"Don't," he said. "Dammit."

"What?"

"That car is following us."

"That's not good. Is it cops or robbers?"

"It's a Lexus, definitely civilian. New plan. Put the laptop back in the bag."

"Done."

Matt turned around and said, "You're going to slide into the driver's seat at the next traffic light."

"Where will you be?"

"I'm going to get out when we stop. Wait two blocks, then pull over. When you get out of the Jeep, there's a giant oak tree there, hide behind it. You're going to take the laptop."

"That's the plan? Run, hide and carry your stuff?"

He winked at Kresley and gave her thigh a squeeze. "Don't worry. I think a personal introduction is in order."

Before she could protest, he was out of the car. Kresley crawled across the gearshift and looked in the rearview as she put her foot on the gas. She had to point her toes to reach the accelerator but that didn't matter when sure enough, the Lexus continued to tail her. She looked for Matt but he'd managed to disappear into a nearby public park.

Two blocks later, Kresley jerked the car into an illegal loading zone, then hoisted the backpack over her shoulder. Walk normally, she told herself. Don't draw attention to yourself.

Walk.

Screw that. Run!

The tree was several feet from the curb with a trunk wide enough to keep her safe. She hoped. She peered around the trunk, watching the Lexus pull over to the curb. A large, heavily muscled man got out of the driver's seat. He was holding something small his right hand, but she couldn't quite see what it was. She did, however, realize that he was closing fast.

Clutching the backpack to her chest, she glanced around for a better hiding place, one she could reach if she ran in a zigzag motion. She didn't remember why that was a good way to run, it just popped into her head. Anything seemed smarter than standing there waiting to be attacked.

Then she heard the click of a switchblade.

The moment he stepped around the tree with the knife in his hand, Kresley's brain started bombarding her with memories. Clear, orderly memories, not the annoying little snippets.

She knew that this was the man who'd come on the yacht and slaughtered everyone. Kresley took a step back. "You don't need the knife," she said. "I think what you're looking for is right here in this backpack." She patted the nylon. "The pictures? Right?"

"I don't know anything about any pictures. I'm just here to finish a job."

"What job?"

"I'm what you might call an exterminator.

Imagine everyone's surprise when we found out you were alive. You're a loose end and loose ends are bad for business."

"Before you go all Ginsu knife on me, exactly how did you find out I was alive?"

"Television," he said with a grunt. "From there it was pretty easy. You make quite an impression on people. Once I spotted you on Queen Street all I had to do was tail you back to the Rose Tattoo. Security was too tight there, so I just had to be patient."

Kresley looked around. They were at the far north end of the park. Several feet from the path and yards from a gray-haired woman walking her dog. With the traffic noise, Kresley realized no one would hear her if she called for help.

The man flipped the knife from hand to hand. "I think we'll do this the slow and painful way. I owe you for fighting back on the yacht."

When he made a move for her, Kresley threw the backpack at him. He swatted it away as he rounded the trunk of the tree. She opened her mouth to scream, but nothing came out. She heard a thud behind her and turned to see Matt between her and the attacker.

"Nice knife," Matt said, holding the gun with the scope in his right hand. "Put it on the ground and step back."

Instead, the guy pulled his hand back, then threw the knife. It went zipping between Matt and Kresley and embedded in the trunk. Muscle guy reached behind him.

"Don't do it," Matt warned.

He didn't listen. He pulled out a gun of his own and before he could even take aim, Matt shot him squarely in the forehead.

"Run," Matt insisted. "Get into the Jeep and go back to my place. I'll handle the cops."

She shook her head. "I can identify this guy as the person who came on the boat and killed everyone. All I need you to get is that bullet from Kendall. I'll just say that I dug it out myself."

Matt tilted his head to one side and gave her an I-so-don't-think-so look. "And gave yourself three stitches underneath your arm while your left hand was slashed and basically useless. The police aren't stupid."

At the sound of sirens, she grabbed up the backpack and started for the Jeep. Suddenly she saw initials on the blade sticking out of the tree. "USCG," Kresley read from the engraving on the blade. "Too long for initials.

"U.S. Coast Guard. You want to move it along?" Matt asked over the blare of emergency cars speeding their way.

"You need to get out of here, fast," Matt used the hem of his shirt to pick up Muscle Man's gun.

"But—" Kresley started to argue, then realized it was too soon to go to the authorities.

"Go!"

Kresley raced to the Jeep and left the scene just as the first police car arrived, blocking the pathway into the park.

Just as she made it to the alleyway between the Rose Tattoo and Matt's apartment, Gabe called and told her to park the Jeep several blocks down in the public garage, then return via the alleyway. He promised to keep an eye on the surveillance cameras to make sure trouble wasn't waiting for her at Matt's place.

Waiting for Matt to return, Kresley practically wore a rut in the carpet pacing back and forth for the better part of three hours. Gabe offered to come keep her company, as did Shelby and Rose. She declined the offers, even though the waiting was making her nuts. If the police found her, she didn't want anyone from the Rose Tattoo getting arrested with her. She was holding her cell phone, practically willing it to ring. She was so desperate she even checked it a few times just to make sure it was working properly.

The bad guys knew she was at the Rose Tattoo. At least the bad guy with the Coast Guard did. That left her feeling a little less safe than she had before. On the plus side, the bad guys knew enough not to breach the security system. On the downside, the police wouldn't care.

Finally Matt showed up.

Without thinking, Kresley ran into his arms. "Thank God you're okay. I've been so worried. Why didn't you call?"

"Because I was being questioned by the police, then driven back here in a cruiser. I didn't think it was prudent to call the woman they're hunting for all over Charleston."

"What did you tell them?"

"I told them he tried to rob me. I identified myself as an FBI agent. Since he pulled a gun I had no alternative but to shoot. There will be administrative stuff when my superiors get the reports, and they confiscated the guy's gun. Other than that, I pretty much got the reciprocal law-enforcement treatment."

"Which is?"

"They'll do a cursory investigation, then declare it a good shoot. I'm not worried."

"So, now what do we do?" she asked.

"About?"

"Learning who the guy was."

"This is how we're going to find out who the dead guy was," he said as he carefully extracted a pair of sunglasses from the front of his shirt. "I just need to find a way to have this dusted for prints and then see if Gabe has a local contact who can run them through IAFIS without letting anyone know why."

"Why?"

"Because I took the guy's sunglasses before the cops came. That's evidence tampering and a few other felonies right there. It's important for us to stay under the radar now. Gabe might know someone with a print kit."

"We don't need a kit," Kresley said. "I used to do this with my kids when I was a teacher. Watch and learn," she teased as she went into the kitchen and came back with two pencils and a very sharp knife. Matt watched as she attempted to whittle away the yellow wooden pencil casings.

"Here," he said, taking the pencil away from her. "With a knife this sharp two hands are really a must."

Matt scraped at the wood, leaving only the thin line of lead. He repeated the action a second time on the other pencil.

"There's a makeup brush in your medicine cabinet, would you get it, please?"

"In my medicine chest?" Matt asked, clearly surprised.

"I just needed a cotton swab and I happened to see a makeup brush belonging to whoever lived here before you, I guess. I need it, so get it please."

She entered the kitchen. First she laid out a brown grocery bag. She put the shaved pencil leads into the blender and after some pulsing, it was full of graphite dust. In the inevitable junk drawer, she found cellophane tape. All she needed now was the brush and Muscle Guy's sunglasses.

"Here," Matt said.

"Thanks. Now the glasses, please."

Matt laid them on the paper. Then he watched, impressed, as Kresley put some of the pencil lead on the makeup brush and in a swirling motion, dusted the glasses carefully, raising several partial prints.

"Where'd you learn to do that?"

"I don't know. Probably from an episode of some detective show."

She transferred the prints to cellophane tape, and then affixed them to individual pages from the notepad by the phone. "Now that we have the prints, what do we do?"

"We? Nothing. Me? Now that I think about it. I'd like to protect Gabe. I'll fax the prints to a friend at Quantico. I can do that from the bedroom."

"Convenient," she said, tapping the excess pencil dust from the makeup brush.

Chapter Fourteen

Smiling, Matt came back into the room. "I have a name. Hal Whiting. Mean anything to you?"

Kresley shook her head. "Not in the least. Wait a minute…was he the guy you…the guy from the yacht?"

"Yep. He's got a long rap sheet." Matt sat next to her on the sofa. His weight caused her to slide into him so her bare arm rubbed against his. She could feel the heat coming off his body as she valiantly tried to focus on Hal Whiting and not on the fact that Matt was so close. Or that he smelled amazingly male. Or that she wanted him like she'd never wanted a man in her life.

"Want to go to bed?"

"What?" It hadn't come out like a question. It was more of a squeaky, high-pitched syllable masquerading as a question.

"When I came out, you looked like you'd zoned out. You must be exhausted."

"No," Kresley answered. "I'm fine. You're the

one who did the running and shooting. All I did was drive and hide."

Matt placed written proof of Hal Whiting's intensive criminal history on the coffee table, then turned, pulling one leg up so his knee touched the back cushions. "I care how you feel. What you're thinking about. It seems like you're getting more and more of your memory back and I'm hoping that's a good thing."

She eyed him cautiously. "Why?"

"You're smart and intuitive."

Kresley gave him kudos for that. Few men bothered to look past her curves and blond hair. One more Pamela Anderson joke and she'd scream. "As are you."

He shook his head. "Not like you. Not naturally. I worked my butt off for Bs and Cs. I'll bet you never got a C in your life."

"I'm sure I did."

Matt reached out to tuck a strand of hair behind her ear. Even that brief contact was enough to make her melt.

Kresley nervously played with a tiny string caught in the weave of the sofa.

"Thank you for trusting me today," he said. "I trust you, too. In case you were wondering."

"After three whole days? I'd think an FBI agent would be more circumspect."

"Why? Don't you believe people can have an instant connection to one another?"

"I don't know. I think I've decided I believe in lust

at first sight." She cast him a sidelong look. "If I have to take a stance, I think two people should at least be in *like* before they're intimate."

Matt stroked the sexy shadow of stubble on his chin. "I like you."

"Very funny." With those light-blue eyes and that black hair he looked bad-boyish. Oh God. Was she actually falling for a man she barely knew? She didn't trust herself, now knowing she'd come within a hair's breadth of marrying a guy who'd been cheating on her.

"There it is," he said, wagging his forefinger near her face.

"What?"

"That look you get every once in a while. You're miffed or confused about something. You've got a horrible poker face, by the way. So why not just tell me what's bothering you?"

"It's irrelevant. Shouldn't we be focusing on Hal the murderer and not on your interpretations of my facial expressions?" Kresley made a production out of twisting her hair into a mass and securing it with a clip at the crown of her head.

"Okay for now, but we're going to revisit this topic," he said, retrieving Hal's file from the table. "He's got…four, five, six arrests for aggravated assault. Some B and Es and one attempted rape."

"Why wasn't he in jail, or prison or set adrift on a raft in the middle of the Atlantic without food or water?"

Matt smiled. "God help the defendant who gets

you on a jury. In answer to your question, plea bargains. Even with arrests going back to the late eighties, the guy served a total of three years. He must have pull someplace. It takes a lot of juice to keep someone with Hal's record out of jail."

"That's unconscionable." She lifted her throbbing, bandaged left hand and wiggled her fingers. "Ouch." The pain was fifty percent injury related and fifty percent her failure to follow Kendall's instructions to exercise her fingers regularly. Her fingers were as fat as sausages. Who knew fingers could gain weight? "So his boss is also the person who's been getting him off."

"Likely."

"Would a Coast Guard person have that kind of clout?"

Matt nodded. "If he or she was high enough on the food chain. Why the Coast Guard?"

"Hal's knife has USCG on the blade. I'm sure you can't get those at the local Wal-Mart."

"Now that Hal's dead, we can't ask him," Matt said without any remorse.

"Right," she said. "If we figure him out, that should lead us back to the person who hired him. Just out of curiosity, how did you know he'd follow me and not you?"

Matt shrugged. The action caused his T-shirt to pull tautly against his chest and abdomen. "Educated guess."

She swallowed hard. "What if you hadn't gotten there in time?"

"I knew what I was doing."

"Yeah, well, he could have used the gun instead of the knife."

"Are you safe and unharmed?"

She nodded, "But—"

"You're safe and the bad guy is dead. Put that in the win column. You have an incredible mouth," Matt said in a low, husky voice that sent a sensual thrill through her entire body.

"Not much of a segue there. When did my mouth become the topic of conversation?

"Because it fascinates me. You fascinate me," he said, and each word rippled though her.

Kresley saw passion in his hooded eyes. This was one of those defining moments. Either she could give in to the pent-up desire in herself or she could get up and go to bed. Alone.

She did get up, but not to go to bed alone. Instead, she lifted her shirt over her head and dropped it on the floor. Without saying a word, Matt rose and removed his shirt. Kresley stepped forward, flattening her hand against his chest, enjoying the strong beat of his heart beneath her touch.

Her eyes roamed boldly over the vast expanse of his broad shoulders, drinking in the sight of his impressive upper body. "Something about you makes my self-control go right out the window."

She looked up at him, relishing the anticipation fluttering in her stomach.

Protected in the circle of his arms, Kresley closed her eyes and rested against his chest, knowing exactly what she needed to do. But not tonight. Tonight she could forget everything. Forget everything but the magic of being with him.

He ignited feelings so powerful and so intense in her that Kresley fleetingly wondered if such sensations were even possible. As he moved the tip of his finger across her taut nipple, she couldn't think any more.

Matt moved his hand in a series of slow, sensual circles until it rested against her rib cage, just under the swell of her breast. He wanted to see the desire in her eyes. Catching her chin between his thumb and forefinger, he tilted her head up with the intention of searching her eyes. He never made it that far.

His eyes were riveted to her lips, which were slightly parted, a glistening shade of pale rose.

Lowering his head, he took a tentative taste. Her mouth was warm and pliant, so was her body, which again pressed urgently against him. His hands roamed purposefully, memorizing every nuance and curve.

He felt his own body respond with an ache, then an almost overwhelming rush of desire surged through him. Kresley's arms slid around his waist, pulling him closer. Matt marveled at the perfect way they fit together. It was as if Kresley had been made for him. For this.

"Kresley," he whispered against her mouth. He toyed with a lock of her hair first, then slowly wound his hand through the silken mass and gave a gentle tug on the clip, forcing her head back even more.

Looking down at her face, Matt knew there was no sight on earth as beautiful and inviting.

Her long, silky blond hair fell down around her bare shoulders.

With a finger, Matt traced the delicate outline of her mouth. Her skin was flawless, with a faint, rosy flush.

He showered her face and neck with light kisses. His mouth searched for that sensitive spot at the base of her throat. A pleasurable moan spilled from his mouth when she began running her palms over the tight muscles of his stomach.

He kissed her for a long time, savoring the slower pace. In one lithe movement, Matt carried her down the hall to the bedroom, then to the bed.

Capturing both of her hands in one of his, he gently held them above her head. The position arched her back, drawing his eyes down to the outline of her erect nipples. "Does this hurt?"

"What?" she asked in a fog of need.

"Me holding your hands. I don't want to hurt the stitches."

"You aren't hurting me, but you are making me crazy. I want to touch you. This isn't playing fair."

"Believe me, it's better for both if us if I don't let you keep touching me," he reassured her with a smile and a kiss.

Kresley responded by lifting her body to him. The rounded swell of one exposed breast brushed his arm. His fingers closed over the rounded fullness.

"Please let me touch you!" Kresley cried out.

"Not yet," he whispered, ignoring her futile struggle to release her hands. He dipped his head to kiss the raging pulse point at her throat. Her soft skin grew hot as he worked his mouth lower and lower. She gasped when his mouth closed around her nipple, then she called his name in a hoarse voice that caused a tremor to run the full length of his body.

Moments later, he lifted his head only long enough to get rid of the rest of their clothing. He wanted to see her passion-laden expression. He told her she was beautiful.

"So are you."

Whether because of the sound of her voice or possibly the way she pressed herself against him, Matt found himself nearly undone by the level of passion Kresley evoked.

He sought her mouth again as he released his hold on her hands and his body covered hers. His hands slid downward, skimming the side of her body all the way to her thighs. Then, giving in to the urgent need pulsing through him, Matt positioned himself between her legs. Every muscle in his body tensed as he looked at her face.

Kresley lifted her hips, welcoming, inviting, as her hands went to his hips and tugged him toward her.

"You're amazing," he groaned against her lips.

"Thank you," she whispered back. "I want you. Now, please?"

He wasted no time responding to her request. In a single motion, he thrust deeply, knowing without question that he had found heaven on earth.

The sheer pleasure of being inside her sweet softness was very powerful. He kept the rhythm of their lovemaking at a slow, deliberate pace, savoring the sensation of her body convulsing.

A long, pleasurable time later, Kresley again wrapped her legs around his hips as explosive waves surged through him. Satisfaction had never been so sweet.

With his head buried next to hers, the sweet scent of her hair filled his nostrils. Matt reluctantly relinquished possession of her body. It took several minutes before his breathing slowed to a steady, satiated pace.

He could have happily stayed next to her in the big soft bed until the end of time. He held her close, sensing when she fell asleep in the cradle of his arm. Before he drifted off himself, he knew she was the one.

Chapter Fifteen

"You know he's going to be mad when he wakes up and you aren't there," Rose said, as Kresley placed her suitcase in the back seat of the woman's oversize car.

"He's a big boy, he'll get over it. I can't let him risk getting more involved," Kresley argued. "I need to do this before I get any of you in trouble. I don't need that guilt on top of what I already feel."

Even in the dark, she had the unmistakable sense that Rose was not pleased. And as expected, Rose didn't hide her displeasure. "I thought you didn't have a memory. If you can't remember anything, why are you feeling guilty?"

Kresley opened the passenger door and got in, cradling a paper bag. "I just am. Would you mind stopping by the morgue? I want to get the bullet from Kendall."

"This isn't a good idea."

"Got a better one?" Kresley asked. "I can't run from the police forever. Matt killed a man to keep me safe yesterday. This is the only solution."

"I heard about the shooting on the local news. Sounds like Matt killed someone who needed killing. That isn't what has you running scared," Rose insisted. "What happened between you and Matt?"

"Too much," Kresley muttered.

Rose patted her lacquered, gravity defying hair. "Until you came along, Matt hasn't shown an interest in anyone. He meets you and he's a different person."

"That's the problem. I don't want to make him different. Until a month ago, I was going to marry a guy. It defies logic to think I could go from loving one guy to lo—then jump into another man's arms, especially when I don't have all the pieces of my life back. Plus, he's got an issue of his own to deal with."

"What issue?" Rose asked.

There was no way Kresley would break his confidence. "He shared something with me. It's not my place to repeat it."

Rose was shaking her head. "Life is complicated. If you have feelings for the man, don't be dumb enough to turn your back on them."

"It's not stupid. I'm protecting him."

"You're running away."

"I'm turning myself in to the police. That's not running away. That's doing the right thing."

"Right for who?" Rose asked when they got to the hospital. She steered her 1958 pink Cadillac into the lot behind the building. One set of shiny double doors seemed to be the only way in or out.

"Stay here. And Kresley?"

"Yes?"

"If you've got some makeup in your bag, use it."

"Thanks." Kresley turned on the interior lights and twisted the rearview mirror to get a look at herself. She'd showered and washed her hair. It was clean but still damp. She didn't have a lick of makeup on.

More to kill time than for vanity's sake, she opened her suitcase and took out some blush, mascara and got a lip gloss from her purse. Okay, so she didn't look like a runway model, but she didn't look like a corpse, either.

Rose came back holding a small plastic screw-top cup with the bullet fragment inside. Odd that such a dangerous thing could jingle like a baby's rattle.

"I called Gabe when I was waiting on Kendall to get the bullet. He's going to meet us a block from the police station."

"Thank you."

"Don't thank me, he thinks you're being an idiot, too, so expect him to talk you out of this silly plan of yours."

Just as they parked to wait for Gabe, Kresley's cell phone rang. Glancing at the caller ID, she ignored the call, then powered off the phone. She didn't have to have a conversation with Matt to know what he'd think of her plan.

After ten minutes, Kresley said, "Maybe he isn't coming."

"He'll be here," Rose insisted. "Give him a little while longer."

The light suddenly dawned. "You called from

inside the morgue so I wouldn't hear what you told Gabe, right? You told him to bring Matt along."

"Kresley, you need people around you who— Where are you going?"

"I'm walking a block with the bullet and the dress and telling the authorities everything I know."

"Kresley, sugar!" Rose called as Kresley exited the car and headed straight for the police headquarters situated in the city's main municipal building.

She took a deep breath, then went inside.

The officer in charge of the conveyer belt and metal detector didn't seem to recognize her. He did, however, recognize a bullet when he saw one.

He purposefully muffled his voice as he spoke into the two-way radio clipped to his shoulder, then said, "Ma'am, I'm going to have to ask you to wait over here."

"Okay," Kresley said, reaching for the paper bag.

The deputy clamped his hand on her wrist. "We'll leave that there for now if you don't mind, miss."

"Don't mind at all." Kresley moved over to the exact floor tile he'd pointed to and waited. The faint smell of coffee was almost lost in the heavy scent of pine cleaner. There were a few muffled conversations, but the acoustics in the large building made it impossible for her to tell which direction the voices were coming from.

Soon three officers, one female in uniform and two males in street clothes came and got her.

"This is Officer Travis and this is Detective Walsh and I'm Detective Peltier."

The female cop, Officer Travis, had her by the arm, Detective Walsh was at her side and Detective Peltier was behind her, carrying the bag.

She was led through a maze of desks to an interrogation room. Officer Travis stood like a sentry in the corner. Detective Walsh pulled out a chair for Kresley and then joined Detective Peltier on the opposite side of the scratched laminate table. The two detectives looked to be in their late thirties, maybe early forties. Walsh was the better looking of the two, his blue eyes reminded her a little bit of Matt.

"Did you know we've been looking for you, Miss Hayes?"

"I saw it on the news, yes."

"You opted to hide from us because…?"

"I've been hoping more of my memory would return so I could be useful to your investigation."

All three of them looked at her skeptically.

"I know," she said, holding up her bandaged hand. "It sounds crazy, unfortunately, it's true. There's still a lot I can't remember."

"Tell us what you can recall," Walsh said.

It took Kresley the better part of an hour to recount the relevant fragments of her life from a few days prior to taking the cruise on the *Carolina Moon,* through what had happened on the yacht, and then she lied her way through the last four days.

They peppered her with question after question. She steadfastly insisted that she'd removed the bullet herself and stitched up her own palm. It was obvious by their expressions that they didn't buy that part of her story. She wouldn't have, either. All the same she wasn't about to implicate anyone from the Rose Tattoo who'd helped her.

"Do you know one of your earrings was found on the yacht?"

She nodded. "I must have lost it during the fight." When she described the muscular man, that seemed to pique the interest of the police.

"A man fitting that description was found in the park last night. Shot during a robbery. Know anything about that?" Peltier asked.

"I didn't shoot him, if that's what you're suggesting."

"No," Travis said. "We know the identity of the shooter. Is it possible that the man who was shot broke in to your apartment?"

"It would make sense that whoever arranged for the murders thinks I got or took or saw something he wanted back and was willing to kill me to get it."

"And who's been helping you?" Peltier asked.

"No one."

He hooted dismissively. "Your landlady told us she saw a tall man with you two days ago."

"She was mistaken," Kresley answered coolly. "Yes, I was at my apartment, however as soon as I saw it had been tossed, I packed a bag and left."

"And the bullet wound? I guess now you're going to tell me you dug it out yourself."

She shrugged. "I didn't think I could go to a hospital. At the time I didn't know who I could trust."

"Remove the bandage on your hand please," Walsh said to Kresley, then to Travis added, "Get an EMT over here now."

Carefully, Kresley removed the bandage, revealing five deep cuts and three minor ones. It wasn't a very pretty sight.

Peltier leaned over for a better look. "Your fingernails are shorter on your left hand."

That was it? He's mocking my manicure?

"Typically that indicates that your left hand is your dominant hand. Are you left-handed, Miss Hayes?"

"Yes."

"Then maybe you can demonstrate with some thread and cloth how you managed to stitch your left hand as well as perform surgery to remove the bullet with your right hand. All of which, I'm assuming, you did without numbing medications."

"Does that matter more than why I was shot? Why I've been getting threatening phone calls and why someone killed Gianni when I was in his shop? Whatever this is, it didn't end on the yacht."

Travis came in with an EMT and Matt. Matt glared at Kresley for a second, then extended his hand to the detectives. His FBI badge dangled from the front pocket of his jeans.

"Special Agent DeMarco, please sit down. Miss Hayes was just regaling us with stories about how she managed to fend off an assassin, swim three miles to shore, perform first aid and surgery all by herself."

"Ouch!" Kresley said as the kneeling EMT brushed something across the stitches in her hand.

"Sorry, ma'am." The EMT looked to the detectives and said, "No signs of infection."

"Check under her arm," Peltier instructed.

Matt came around and placed a hand on her right shoulder while the EMT examined her wound.

"No infection. Stitches look good."

The EMT was dismissed. Kresley had a difficult time focusing on the two officers across from her because Matt's thumb was slowly stroking her collarbone.

"We can fill in some of the blanks for you," Walsh said. "We had an informant on that yacht. She was killed."

Kresley head was spinning. "But the other women were my roommates."

"Yes, Emma Rooper agreed to wear a wire in exchange for a dismissal of all charges."

"So that's why Emma said she was sorry," Kresley thought aloud. "You have everything on tape? What were the charges?"

"In addition to facilitating the cocaine transfers from and to the yacht, Emma was also laundering money for Declan Callaghan. We had every expectation that Declan would implicate himself on the last run. However, the recorder was missing when we recovered Emma's body."

"But Emma didn't put the tape recorder on me," Kresley mumbled.

"What?"

Kresley described the tall woman with the short brown hair, who she now presumed was Janice, taping a recording device to her rib cage. "Any chance I was working for you, too?"

"You were just a last-minute addition," Walsh said. "Apparently Declan had Emma bring along another woman because there would be a fourth man aboard. It was very important that it look like a romantic cruise around the harbor."

"What was the show?" Kresley asked.

"I don't follow," Peltier said.

"I remember a blond man telling me to go to the port side of the ship so I didn't miss the show."

"Do you remember what time this was?"

"Around two hours after we boarded."

"On the same nights the yacht went out, one of Declan's shell corporations rented a barge and shot off fireworks in the harbor."

"So the fireworks were a cover?" Matt asked. "They waited for the guests to be on the opposite side of the boat so they could off-load cocaine?"

"Cocaine off, weapons on," Walsh said. "Seems Declan has a new partner who prefers to deal in arms. We think Foxy R is the middle man, but so far, we haven't been able to link him. Emma was supposed to get Declan on tape naming his partners."

"When did Declan get this new partner?" Matt asked.

"A couple of months ago. We were hoping that Miss Hayes saw something or heard something, that's why we released her photo to the press."

"Well, you very nearly got me killed," Kresley said. "Is there a link between the Coast Guard and any drug smuggling and arms sales?"

"We've got a liaison with them and the harbor police. We had to. Couldn't risk them going too close to the yacht before we got hard evidence."

"Drugs and weapons aren't evidence?" Kresley asked.

"You have to look at the broader picture, Miss Hayes. Yes, we could have boarded the yacht and confiscated the cocaine. Everyone on board would be arrested for trafficking. I can promise you though, that before we'd finished booking everyone, Declan's partner would already have a replacement in place. We couldn't move in until we knew all the players."

"Okay," Kresley said, seeing the logic. She stood up. "Well, if there's nothing else."

"Who knows you came here?"

"Four people, possibly five." She glanced at Matt and it made her heart squeeze. "If you told Shelby."

"I did."

"Then five," she told the detectives.

"Then you could be very useful to us, Miss Hayes."

"Oh hell, no," Matt said. "You are not using her as bait."

"I won't kid you, this isn't without its risks," Peltier said.

"It's nothing but risks," Matt yelled. He reached for Kresley's arm, but she pulled it back.

"These people are going to continue to try to kill me until you catch them, right?"

The detectives nodded. Matt cupped her face in his hands and said, "You don't have to do this. There are other ways for them to catch Declan and flush out his partner."

Kresley all but slapped his hands away. "I'll do it."

"No, you won't," Matt said emphatically. "Could we have the room for a few minutes?" The detectives hesitated. "Look, we all know that Declan has interests in several states. One phone call and I can have the FBI take jurisdiction. I'd rather just have a few minutes with Miss Hayes."

Under the threat of losing their case, they filed out and Kresley leaned against the wall, arms crossed. Matt started toward her and she held out her hand. "That's close enough."

"Did I miss something?" Matt asked. "We made love last night. You fell asleep in my arms. Then I get up and find you gone? What happened? When did this go wrong?"

"It didn't," she assured him with a sad smile. "I did."

"I'm lost. Tell me what you did?"

"You were like some prince who rode in on the proverbial white horse, saving me from danger. Because of me, you killed a man. There's no balance. Nothing I can give you. Nothing to offer. I'm too dependent on you, Matt."

"How can you say that? As you're so fond of telling me, we haven't known each other long enough. By the way, that's your take, not mine. I knew you were the one the first time I saw your face."

Kresley hung her head for a moment. "Look, Matt. I appreciate everything you did for me but I'm going to do whatever the police need me to do so I can have my life back."

"Fine. At least let me help you."

"I think you've helped me enough."

"Okay, so we'll have new rules. Slow things down. No touching, no sex, just getting to know each other. Work for you?"

She hated that she couldn't keep from smiling. "It might."

"Then we have a deal."

Chapter Sixteen

"It almost looks normal," Kresley said as she stood in the center of her living room. Some things had been repaired while others required replacement. All on the Charleston PD's dime. Oh, and there were some other alterations, as well. There were cameras secreted in every room except the bathroom and a door hidden by a screen that led to the adjacent apartment where the police would be watching over her every hour of the day.

The other major change was no Matt. Only phone calls for the past eleven days. If this was going to work, the cops didn't want Matt's presence to put Declan's partner off. His new partner needed to find himself another shooter for hire, and fast.

Hearing someone knocking on the door, Kresley felt a surge of panic. Since the cops always called before one of them came over, she was unnerved, to put it mildly, by any unannounced visitor.

"Who is it?" she called, standing off to the side as the police instructed. Apparently hit men often fired through doors so it was never a good idea to stand directly forward.

"It's Gabe," the person on the other side of the door called out. She relaxed immediately and rushed to the door. Opening it, she smiled at him. "How are you?"

"Fine. Nice place," he said, glancing around as he shifted a heavy-looking cooler to the other hand.

"The setup is that I'm looking for roommates," she said. "The police will cover the rent while their investigation is ongoing."

"I'll keep that in mind if my wife tosses me out."

"Want me to take that?" she asked, nodding to the cooler.

"I'll leave it in the kitchen."

She offered him a seat on the sofa. "What are you doing here?" She flushed. "That didn't come out right. It's nice to see a friendly face, but I thought everyone was told to stay away."

"I got a hall pass from the detectives."

"Would you get one for me? The only time they allow me to leave is to get the newspaper and the mail. Something about keeping to a schedule so if someone's watching, they'll learn my routine."

Gabe's hazel eyes narrowed. "Are you still sure this is a good idea?"

"Mostly. My memory is a lot better. You can quiz me on my childhood if you want." She held up her hand. "They took the stitches out yesterday. My palm resembles the bride of Frankenstein, but everything is healing nicely. I'm babbling, huh?"

"A little," he said with a smile.

"How's Matt?"

"He's walking around looking like someone just killed his favorite dog."

"We talk on the phone every night but with my, um, friends in the other room listening in, it's kind of inhibiting."

"He's working around the clock."

"I'd love more to do. I've caught up on my course work and even gotten ahead."

"I know it's tough but if someone is watching this place, seeing a federal agent walking through the door is sure to spook them." He checked his watch. "My allotted time is up. The cooler is a gift from Rose, Shelby and pretty much everyone at the Rose Tattoo. We figured you were probably sick of soup and pizza."

"You have no idea," Kresley said with a sigh.

Gabe's short visit only made her feel more isolated. Maybe agreeing to work with the Charleston PD was a mistake, especially when everything felt so open-ended. For all she knew, eleven days could turn into eleven months.

She grabbed a novel and tried to read. Then she tried listening to her iPod. When her cell phone rang, she excitedly answered, expecting Matt.

"Hello."

"Be on the three-thirty harbor tour today. If you don't show, I'll have no choice but to go out for a drink with your *friend*." The female voice was distorted, but familiar. Frustratingly, Kresley still couldn't place it. Her meaning, however, was crystal-clear.

The detectives appeared at her door in under a second, buoyed that someone had finally made contact.

"Foxy R has several girls working for him," Walsh told her.

"Prostitutes?" Kresley clarified.

He nodded. "Makes sense he'd use one of them to make contact."

"I guess in this economy it's probably good to diversify," Kresley said nervously as she looked at her watch and felt the seed of terror germinating.

She had less than thirty minutes to make it to the pier. "We need to hurry if I'm going to make it to the pier on time." She grabbed up her purse and began digging for her keys.

"We're not going," Walsh said. "It's not an environment we can secure on such short notice."

"I'm going," Kresley said. "That wasn't idle chatter about having a drink. She was telling me that if I didn't show up, Matt would be the new target."

Walsh grabbed her upper arm. "I can't sanction this, Miss Hayes."

"Well, I can't risk anything happening to Matt."

"We can call him," the detective argued. "We'll bring him in and put him in a safe location until this is resolved."

Somehow Kresley knew Matt would never agree to lay low while she remained a target. She pulled her arm free. "I'm going. Follow me, don't follow me. I couldn't care less."

She had her keys in one hand and was digging for her cell phone as she jogged for her car. Focused on calling Matt to warn him, she was only vaguely aware of the two detectives trailing her.

"Rose Tattoo, how may I help you?"

"Hi, Susan," Kresley said as she tossed her purse on the passenger's seat, then stuck the keys in the ignition in nearly a single motion. "I need to talk to Matt."

"He's not here," she said.

"Gabe said he was working today."

"He was until about five minutes ago. He ran out of here like he was being chased by the devil himself."

Kresley's heart sank, remembering he'd cloned her phone. She gunned the engine and screeched tires as she exited the parking lot.

She tried Matt's cell, weaving erratically through traffic. One glance in the mirror and she spotted the two unmarked cars following in succession.

Her heart was thumping by the time she reached the pier.

As she stood in line with the tourists, she repeatedly called Matt's cell phone, irritated when it kept going to voice mail.

"Could you move up please, miss?"

Turning, Kresley realized that a deckhand was stringing a rope across he gangway. The police weren't going to make the cut, so Kresley started to turn around when the tall woman in a yellow dress and a large-brimmed straw hat standing in front of her in line suddenly stuck something hard in her ribs.

"Oh, you're going to get off the boat, Kresley. And this time, I'll make damned sure you aren't breathing when you hit the water."

FROM THEIR vantage point on the observation deck, Matt and Gabe had an unobstructed view of the gangway.

Matt was silent for a minute as he processed the sight of Janice holding a gun on Kresley. "I never would have believed it."

"Yeah, well, considering that her police detail didn't make it aboard, I'm grateful you heard the call."

"When Kresley suggested it might be Janice I dismissed the idea," Matt said as he lifted his binoculars. "Janice has a SIG-Sauer in her right hand and judging by the way she's standing, I'm guessing she has a .22 in a thigh holster."

"Could be Janice's using Kresley to get close to Declan."

Matt shifted the binoculars out of the way and looked over at Gabe. "Janice would never need another woman to get close to a man."

"What do you want to do?" Gabe asked.

"We can't let this boat leave the dock. Get the captain to stay put and if he won't listen, call the Coast Guard. I'm going after Kresley."

Matt struggled past the passengers coming up the stairs, racing to get to the gangway before Janice took Kresley and disappeared into the bowels of the eighty-foot-long tour boat.

He kept the Glock in his hand pressed against his leg so he wouldn't alarm the tourists. The last thing he needed right now was a mob of screaming passengers rushing the gangway. With four steps left, he watched Janice poke Kresley with the gun, pointing her toward a hatch labeled Employees Only. He was on the bottom step when his cell phone began vibrating in his pocket. Glancing down at his cell, he saw that it was Kresley calling as the two women stepped through the hatch. He listened in to their conversation as he continued to push toward them.

"Calling me at seven-twenty. That and getting Declan on tape were your only jobs," Janice said, her voice dripping with venom.

"Even without the tape, by now you must have enough to build a strong case against him," Kresley said, trying to stall for time, hoping that Matt was listening in and was somewhere near.

"I had a case against Declan months ago. Funny thing though, I discovered I liked his lifestyle a lot more than my own. And no one raked me over the coals if I showed…initiative," she said bitterly.

"So you went from federal agent to drug smuggler?"

Janice shook her head. "That's far too pedestrian. Hal Whiting brought in the cocaine, which he sold to Foxy R. Foxy sold it on the streets and used the profits to buy guns. Guns he purchased through offshore corporations owned by Declan. Very industrious and very lucrative."

Kresley paused for a moment, letting it all sink in as she remembered how Janice had approached her. How naive she'd been, buying Janice's story about needing one more bit of evidence to make her case, and giving her $10,000 to do it. No, *naive* wasn't the right work, *blind* was. She was desperate for money and had allowed Janice to persuade her it was FBI sting money.

And how naive had her roommates been, too, taking $10,000 payments as she'd learned, simply for being dinner escorts on alleged romantic cruises. And they'd paid with their lives.

"What, then, did you need me for?"

"I needed to know when Declan got off the boat so I could board it and take the cocaine before the Coast Guard showed up and beat me to it. The blood bath would have been unnecessary if you'd just done your little job. No, instead of implicating Declan on tape to get me leverage, you ended up implicating me. His voice was on that tape, but so was mine."

"So you shot me?" Kresley asked, a tremble in her voice.

"Of course, you didn't think I was going to allow you to swim to shore with that recorder taped to your chest. Not that it makes any difference, but did you really lose it?"

Matt carefully stepped through the hatch. The darkness was a stark contrast to the blinding sunlight. He shifted the gun, flicked the safety off and stood listening to their conversation. He noticed the hallway split at the next hatch and with the echo, he didn't know which way Janice would go.

"Yes, I did," Kresley said defiantly. "A night bobbing in the ocean can do that."

Janice slapped Kresley hard across the face.

Kresley wiped at the blood in the corner of her mouth. "Why are you taking me to the engine room?"

"Thank you, sweetheart," Matt muttered as he ran through the passageways until he found the engine room. He entered, then crouched down and held the door until it closed soundlessly. The room was deafeningly loud due to the numerous chugging pistons and routers.

"See, no one is here," Janice said. "That's the thing with these new ships. They're all computer-controlled from the bridge. We're all alone."

"Killing me won't serve any purpose. I don't have the tape. I can't remember most of what happened on the yacht," Kresley said, praying that Janice believed that.

"Wrong. It will do me good. It will prove to Declan that I am a capable and useful partner to have. I've already proved that there were too many people in the chain. Enough talking, get on your knees."

"I think I prefer to be looking at you when you shoot me," Kresley said.

"Suit yourself."

Kresley spun around with enough force to deliver a roundhouse kick that sent Janice's gun sailing.

Even disarmed, Matt knew that Janice remained a threat. He stood and ran full out, reaching them just as Janice used the metal railings to lift herself up and get Kresley in a headlock between her knees.

Kresley's face was flushed and her eyes bulged. Matt grabbed Janice in a chokehold and squeezed until she went completely limp.

Gabe burst through the door, gun drawn. Just in time to see Kresley step over Janice and fall into Matt's waiting arms.

"ARE YOU SURE nothing hurts?"

"Positive," Kresley said for the umpteenth time. "You can put me down any time."

"I'll put you down once we're inside."

True to his word, Matt set her down on the sofa so carefully it was as if she were made of glass. Almost immediately, his mouth found hers and they kissed for a long, blissful time. Kresley's mind was so muddled with desire that it took a second for her to process the pounding sound. When she reluctantly pulled away from Matt someone was banging on the door.

"Matthew DeMarco, you open this door right now!"

"She won't go away," Kresley said with a smile. "Might as well let her in."

Rose was standing with her hands on her hips. Shelby was right behind her. She pushed Matt aside and walked in. "Well, thank God you aren't hurt," Rose said. She turned to Matt. "What you and Gabe did was stupid and dangerous."

"She's right," Kresley opined, enjoying the way Rose just chastised men twice her size without so much as blinking. Shelby stepped past them and joined Kresley on the sofa. "Are you sure you're okay? We can have a doctor here in—"

"I'm fine," Kresley insisted. "A couple of bruises, but no blood. I did break a nail though."

Shelby smiled. "I'm glad you're not hurt."

"We're all glad," Rose said in her uniquely abrupt manner. "You two have exactly one hour to do…*whatever,* then I expect you at the restaurant."

"Rose," Matt began reasonably. "It's been a really long day and—"

"And what? You can't eat? We're closing the place down for the night. Family only."

"Then maybe I shouldn't—"

"Yes, you should," Shelby cut in. "You don't have any family. You could do worse than all of us."

Kresley felt honored and for the first time in a long time, she felt she belonged somewhere.

Matt looked over his shoulder and caught her eye. "Mind if I go talk to Shelby for a few minutes?"

Kresley shook her head and offered an encouraging smile.

"Finally," Shelby said, and she walked over and wrapped her arms around Matt. "I already know you're my half brother."

"I sensed it!" Rose said with a satisfied clap of her hands. "The two of you look too much alike."

Matt stepped back. Kresley could only see his profile. He looked…*baffled*. "How did you know?"

Shelby laughed. "Dylan told me."

"He said he'd give me two weeks to tell you myself."

Shelby patted his arms. "Good, I get to share some sisterly advice right off the bat. Dylan and I don't have any secrets. We made that mistake once and it cost us a lot. Don't make the same mistake I did."

"One hour," Rose said, ushering Shelby out the door. "Don't make me walk all the way back here."

"We won't," Kresley answered.

"Why are you smiling?" Matt asked as he rejoined her on the sofa.

"C'mon, it's pretty amusing that you've been creeping around trying to keep a secret when Shelby knew from the get-go," Kresley teased.

"How was I supposed to know that Dylan lied to my face?"

"You were a stranger and she's his wife? It was probably a no-brainer for him to chose which one of you to lie to."

"Good point," he said, nuzzling her neck. "The ballistics are back on your bullet."

"Since we're on a truth thing, telling me I have my own bullet is not conducive to seduction. I'm not so sure I like having my own bullet."

He kissed her earlobe, then laughed as he pulled back so their eyes met. "It matched the slug they got out of Gianni and that means Janice killed him, likely because once the police spoke to him about the gowns, he would have identified her."

"Okay. So, what happens now?"

"There might be a trial, although I think Janice and Declan will have a race to see who can cut the better deal. Then—"

"Not that. This. Us."

He cradled her face with his hands and kissed her softly. "I'm ready and willing to play by your rules. It would be nice if you'd give me some hint about how long this getting-to-know-you thing has to last."

Kresley checked her watch. "Another sixty seconds should do it."

"Really?" he asked, peppering her face with kisses. "How much longer?"

"Thirty seconds."

"Are you sure your watch didn't stop?"

"Just replaced the battery. Ten seconds."

"Who knew a minute could take this long?"

"Time's up," she said.

"Finally. I love you and I want to marry you."

"I love you and I want to marry you, too, but you live in Virginia and I live here."

"I thought you might bring that up," he said, reaching into his back pocket and producing a business card. "Here."

She took the card and read, "Langston and DeMarco, Investigations."

"You and Gabe are going into business together?"

"Yes."

"And what if I'd said no?"

"I figured I could wait you out or wear you down," he whispered as he claimed her mouth, picked her up and carried her to the bedroom.

* * * * *

Celebrate 60 years of pure reading pleasure with Harlequin® Books!

Harlequin Romance® is celebrating by showering you with DIAMOND BRIDES *in February 2009.*
Six stories that promise to bring a touch of sparkle to your life, with diamond proposals and dazzling weddings, sparkling brides and gorgeous grooms!

Enjoy a sneak peek at Caroline Anderson's TWO LITTLE MIRACLES, available February 2009 from Harlequin Romance®.

'I'VE FOUND HER.'

Max froze.

It was what he'd been waiting for since June, but now—now he was almost afraid to voice the question. His heart stalling, he leaned slowly back in his chair and scoured the investigator's face for clues. 'Where?' he asked, and his voice sounded rough and unused, like a rusty hinge.

'In Suffolk. She's living in a cottage.'

Living. His heart crashed back to life, and he sucked in a long, slow breath. All these months he'd feared—

'Is she well?'

'Yes, she's well.'

He had to force himself to ask the next question. 'Alone?'

The man paused. 'No. The cottage belongs to a man called John Blake. He's working away at the moment, but he comes and goes.'

God. He felt sick. So sick he hardly registered the

next few words, but then gradually they sank in. 'She's got *what?*'

'Babies. Twin girls. They're eight months old.'

'Eight—?' he echoed under his breath. 'They must be his.'

He was thinking out loud, but the P.I. heard and corrected him.

'Apparently not. I gather they're hers. She's been there since mid-January last year, and they were born during the summer—June, the woman in the post office thought. She was more than helpful. I think there's been a certain amount of speculation about their relationship.'

He'd just bet there had. God, he was going to kill her. Or Blake. Maybe both of them.

'Of course, looking at the dates, she was presumably pregnant when she left you, so they could be yours, or she could have been having an affair with this Blake character before…'

He glared at the unfortunate P.I. 'Just stick to your job. I can do the math,' he snapped, swallowing the unpalatable possibility that she'd been unfaithful to him before she'd left. 'Where is she? I want the address.'

'It's all in here,' the man said, sliding a large envelope across the desk to him. 'With my invoice.'

'I'll get it seen to. Thank you.'

'If there's anything else you need, Mr Gallagher, any further information—'

'I'll be in touch.'

'The woman in the post office told me Blake was

away at the moment, if that helps,' he added quietly, and opened the door.

Max stared down at the envelope, hardly daring to open it, but when the door clicked softly shut behind the P.I., he eased up the flap, tipped it and felt his breath jam in his throat as the photos spilled out over the desk.

Oh, lord, she looked gorgeous. Different, though. It took him a moment to recognise her, because she'd grown her hair, and it was tied back in a ponytail, making her look younger and somehow freer. The blond highlights were gone, and it was back to its natural soft golden-brown, with a little curl in the end of the ponytail that he wanted to thread his finger through and tug, just gently, to draw her back to him.

Crazy. She'd put on a little weight, but it suited her. She looked well and happy and beautiful, but oddly, considering how desperate he'd been for news of her for the past year—one year, three weeks and two days, to be exact—it wasn't only Julia who held his attention after the initial shock. It was the babies sitting side by side in a supermarket trolley. Two identical and absolutely beautiful little girls.

* * * * *

When Max Gallagher hires a P.I. to find his estranged wife, Julia, he discovers she's not alone—she has twin baby girls, and they might be his. Now workaholic Max has just two weeks to prove that he can be a wonderful husband and father to the family he wants to treasure.